THE PEWTER PLATE

The Pewter Plate

BY

Florence Parker Simister

ILLUSTRATED BY

LLOYD COE

HASTINGS HOUSE, PUBLISHERS, NEW YORK

y

Library of Congress Catalog Card Number: 57-10735

Published simultaneously in Canada by
S. J. Reginald Saunders, Publishers, Toronto 2B

Printed in the United States of America

FOR MY HUSBAND

WITHOUT WHOSE HELP THERE WOULD BE NO BOOK.

AND FOR MY PARENTS

WITHOUT WHOSE CARE THERE WOULD BE NO WRITER.

Contents

THE PEWTER PLATE

PART ONE *Spring, 1778*

CHAPTER ONE

". . . and Called It Macaroni"

Hannah Williams was still quite a way from the house when she heard a man's voice calling. From that distance it sounded like the chairmender so she did not hurry.

When Hannah was very young, she ran to see the chairmender, but now that she was ten years old she knew there were more exciting things in the world.

So she crossed the field slowly, glad to be walking in the spring sunshine. She could feel the warmth of it through the ruffled cap on her head and the cloak over her shoulders.

In one hand Hannah carried the horsetail rushes she had just gathered near the brook. With these she was going to polish all the pewter on the dresser in the kitchen. There were so few pretty things in the kitchen and Hannah was so fond of pretty things that she liked to polish the pewter and leave it shining as bright as silver. Most of all, she liked to polish her own lovely pewter plate, a birthday present from her aunt Abigail in Newport, her mother's sister.

As Hannah came nearer to the house, she heard the man's voice again, and she knew then that it was not the chairmender. But who was it, she wondered, and what was he calling? Then Hannah heard a loud clatter and the shouts of children. She quickened her steps and as she turned into Green Lane, where she lived, she saw a cart, a handcart, piled with . . .

Hannah blinked and pushed her fine brown hair back from her forehead. The cart was piled high with pewter!

Hannah ran closer. She stared. There were tankards there, and platters, and porringers, and plates.

What did it mean?

The children hopped around the cart, shoving each other, shouting and pointing to the pewter.

"Those are ours," said one.

"That platter is my mother's," said another.

"They are not yours any more," said a boy. "They belong to the gov-ern-ment!"

Hannah felt her heart leap in fear. With one hand she picked up her skirts from around her ankles and ran up the lane to the house. She burst into the kitchen where her mother sat churning butter. Hannah looked at the dresser. In one glance she saw that the pewter was still there: the porringers hanging from hooks along the edge of the top shelf, the pewter plates on the shelf below, the tankards on the bottom shelf.

She crossed the room to where her mother sat. Her words tumbled over each other, she spoke so fast.

"Mother, there is a cart down Green Lane piled with pewter. What is it? Who does the pewter belong to?"

Hannah's mother moved the plunger up and

down in the butter churn.

"It is everybody's pewter," she said quietly, calmly. "The government is collecting it to be melted down for bullets for the war."

"Melt the pewter for bullets?" Hannah's voice was high and shrill.

Her mother reached out with her left hand and took a fold of Hannah's skirt between her fingers and pulled her closer. "Sit down, Hannah," she said. "Sit on the stool here."

Hannah tore herself free. "No!" she shrieked. "No! You will tell me our pewter will be put on the cart. Is that it? All our pewter?"

"All my pewter," her mother answered. "Bullets are needed by our troops to fight the British. Pewter can be melted and made into bullets, so that is why they collect it. But we give it only if we want to, Hannah. You do not have to give your plate from Aunt Abigail."

Hannah's face was red. "I will *not* give it!" she shouted. She remembered the very day her aunt had bought her the plate. They had gone on an errand to Long Wharf and had stopped to look in the window of Mr. Jones' shop at the "Sign of the Pewter Platter." Then, unexpectedly, her aunt

had gone into the shop and bought her the plate. The lovely plate with a lion on the bottom and the name: Gershom Jones.

The girl turned toward her mother and there was grief in her voice. "There are so few pretty things here," she wailed. "How can they take the pewter? How can they? How *can* they?"

She stamped her foot and ran over to the dresser. She picked up her plate. Then she pushed past her mother and ran up the stairs to the little room where she slept. Quickly she opened the chest near the bed and thrust her plate under the petticoats and bonnets and shifts that she kept there. Then she ran back down the stairs.

"I have hidden my plate," she announced loudly, angrily. "They will not have *my* plate. I will not give it."

Hannah's mother was standing near the door to the lane. She turned her head slightly. "Very well," she said quietly. "Sit down now. The cart is here."

Hannah had been so distracted that she had not heard the cart nor the sound of the children's voices coming nearer and nearer up the steep lane. But now they were there, outside the door, near the buttonwood tree. A man was at the door.

"Pewter?" he asked, his hat in his hand.

Hannah's mother nodded toward the dresser.

"All of it?" asked the man.

"Yes," said Hannah's mother. Her blue eyes flashed and her cheeks became pink. "It is for a good cause: for our independence."

"For our independence," the man repeated, and took the porringers off the hooks and the plates and the tankards from the shelves.

Dazed by what was happening, Hannah stood watching. As if walking in her sleep, she followed the man to the door.

Outside, he put the pewter in the cart. The children cheered and counted as he added each piece to the heap already there. Then the cart and the man and the children moved off up Green Lane.

Still Hannah stood at the door, watching until the cart disappeared from sight. Only then did she realize that she still clutched in her hand the horse-tail rushes she had gathered for polishing the pewter.

Hannah stared at them. Slowly she opened her fingers and let the rushes drop to the floor. Then she put her head against the doorframe and cried as if her heart would break.

Across the kitchen Hannah's mother watched her, a sad look on her face, but she did not go near her daughter. She left her alone.

A robin sang in the buttonwood tree. In the corner of the kitchen the tall clock ticked. The plunger in the butter churn made a steady sound as her mother moved it up and down, up and down.

Soon Hannah's sobs came further and further apart. Gradually she stopped crying, and at last she turned to face her mother.

"I don't understand," she said in a dull voice. "Are we wrong and must we be punished by the British?"

Hannah's mother spoke in a firm voice. "No, we are not wrong. We are right, it is the British who are wrong! We *must* be independent and free!" She paused for a moment, then continued in a softer voice, "Can you imagine, Hannah, what it must be like to be in Newport, where Aunt Abigail lives, with the British occupying the town? Here in Providence life is hard enough in wartime, but at least we do not have the British right on top of us!" She thrust the plunger in the churn down hard on the word *British*. "And so we give our pewter to be melted down for bullets. That way we have a share in the War for Independence!"

Hannah caught her breath in one last sob. "Our share is to give away a whole garnish of pewter?" she asked.

"Yes. If it is helpful to the cause, then I will have a feeling of satisfaction, a feeling that I have taken part in the struggle."

Her mother's voice seemed to vibrate in the kitchen for a moment, then it died away, and Hannah heard a bell in the distance. She and her mother both listened, for a bell in these times could mean many things: a fire, an alarm, a victory.

Again, closer, the bell! Now Hannah could faintly hear a voice calling with each clang of it, "Hear ye! Hear ye!"

"The Town Crier!" she said.

"What dreadful thing has happened now?" her mother asked. Then she added, "Run, Hannah, run. He will surely stop in front of the Eagle Inn. Run and hear what it is."

So Hannah picked up her skirts from around her ankles and ran as fast as she could down the narrow, stony lane. From all the lanes around and from all the houses people joined her. Down the hill to the bottom they ran to the Eagle, the inn on the Towne

Street where the stagecoaches came. There a crowd had gathered. It was made up of women, children, and men, and even soldiers in the uniform of the Continental Army.

"Hear ye! Hear ye!" called the Crier, unrolling his proclamation. His voice boomed. "The House of Bourbon in France has entered into an alliance with the State of the thirteen United Provinces in consequence of which Mr. Franklin has been presented to the King of France in quality of Ambassador."

Hannah covered her ears at the shout that went up from the crowd. It must be good news, she thought, although I don't understand it. She turned to run back up the hill to tell her mother, but Mrs. Smith, a family friend, stopped her.

"There will be more, Hannah," said Mrs. Smith. "Wait and hear it all."

Hannah waited, and sure enough the Town Crier read again. "Hear ye! Hear ye! All men and boys over sixteen, anxious to serve their country, will gather on the Town Parade this evening."

Hannah felt a hand drop on her shoulder. She turned. It was her brother, John. His face was flushed, his eyes were shining, and his hair seemed more unruly than usual.

"I'm not over sixteen," he whispered in her ear, "but I am going to the Town Parade this evening."

Hannah looked at him. It was the second time that day the war had come so close. Her mind stopped in fear. Then she thought, Mother will not let him. He's just bragging.

John seemed to read her thoughts, for he cried, "I don't care what Mother and Father say. I am going to the Town Parade this evening. I want to fight for my country. I want to help win this war! Come along home."

Hannah turned to follow him. The Crier was walking northward now, to the Market House and the Church. The people were leaving. They had all heard the news, part of it good, part frightening.

The fright stayed with Hannah as they climbed the hill. But then, she thought, Newport is a long way off. Surely the British can't get to Providence. She said it out loud.

"John? Can the British get to Providence?"

"Of course, they can get to Providence." John sounded impatient, as he usually did with his sister. "Why do you think our people built that fort on Fox Hill? And others in the town? In case the

British come!"

This was a new thought to Hannah. She had known the British were in Newport. She knew it was war. But she never thought that her home would be in the midst of the war. She felt then that she had to run home to see if everything was there—her mother, the house, the garden.

She left John and ran as fast as she could up the hill. As she came to the buttonwood tree, she saw the house sitting in the sunshine. The top half of the door was open and through it she could see the kitchen with its whitewashed walls, the scrubbed table, the chairs. The brass bed-warmer leaned against the fireplace wall and shone where the sunlight touched it. Nearby hung the bellows and the tongs. Faintly, across the kitchen, she could see the door to the borning room, where she and John had been born, where her mother and father slept now. This was her home. How peaceful it looked! It didn't seem possible that the British meant to harm it.

Her mother looked up when she came in. Her voice was sharp and anxious. "Yes? What is it?"

"The French have done something good, and a Mr. Franklin has gone to see the King of France,"

Hannah explained. "I didn't understand it all, but everyone cheered."

A look of relief came over her mother's face and she smiled. "Oh, then they have decided to recognize the thirteen United Colonies and they are going to help us. I thought they were going to. That *is* good news."

She seemed so pleased that Hannah couldn't tell her the second piece of news, about John. That could wait until evening. Her mother would find out about it soon enough.

So they settled down to their tasks. There was no scouring of the pewter, but there were other chores with which Hannah helped. All afternoon she tried not to look at the dresser. She could not bear to see the empty shelves because her heart ached for the pewter.

Sometimes Hannah and her mother talked together, about the war, about the pewter. Sometimes they were silent. And even silence, when it came, lay between them full of love and understanding.

Soon the stew was simmering in the big iron pot hanging from the crane in the fireplace and the room smelled of meat and vegetables. Later Hannah's father came home from a meeting of the

Council of War at the State House and then John, from the fields in back of the house where he had been working.

They all sat down at the table, over which Hannah had spread a cloth. She brought a basin filled with stew and the spoons and forks and knives and some old wooden plates. There was bread baked in the oven in the fireplace and butter churned by her mother. It was a good supper, and when it was almost over John scraped back his chair and said nervously, "Father, the Town Crier was at the Eagle Inn this afternoon when you were at the State House."

"I know," said his father. "He brought news of the French Treaty."

"Yes, but also he said for men and boys over sixteen to report to the Town Parade this evening."

Hannah looked at her mother, for she had made a small sound. Her face had turned pale. She said to Hannah reprovingly, "You didn't tell me that."

Hannah whispered, "I couldn't, Mother, because John . . ."

John interrupted, "Because I told Hannah that I want to go!" He blurted it out. "And I *do* want to. I'm almost sixteen, Father. May I go? I *want* to!"

Hannah's mother leaned anxiously toward her husband. "Richard? You will not let him?"

Hannah's father sat quietly for a moment and then he said, "I think I *must* let him. We need all the troops we can raise."

Hannah's mother asked, "Is that what the Council of War decided?"

"Yes," answered her father. "We must raise more troops. Perhaps there will be a battle."

"A battle?" John's voice was full of excitement. "Where, Father? Here?"

"Not here, John, if by here you mean Providence. But close by, perhaps."

Hannah's mother got up from her chair and took John's plate. "There's a pie, John. Will you have some?" Her voice was quiet, almost normal, but Hannah felt that something was the matter with her.

John stood up. "No, Mother. No pie for me. I must go. Father does his share at the foundry and by being a member of the Council of War. I must do mine."

Hannah's mother turned and now Hannah could see what was wrong—the tears were standing like raindrops in her eyes. "But Father's a *man*," she said. "This is a man's business, this war."

Hannah's father rose and went to his wife. He put his hand on her arm. "Martha," he said, and his voice was the kindest Hannah ever remembered it, "John is a man. He is only a few months short of being sixteen. In these days sixteen is a man."

Hannah felt a tear fall on her hand and was surprised to find that *she* was crying, too. The stew on her plate suddenly became tasteless. She got up and started to take away the dishes.

John walked to the fireplace and looked up at the gun and the powder horn hanging over the mantel. "May I take your musket, Father?"

Hannah's father looked at the gun and at John. "Come back after you enlist," he said. "I'll have it ready."

Hannah spoke. "Will you come back tonight, John?"

"I think so. I'm just going to enlist. Mother?" He walked over to her. "Mother, you're not angry?"

Hannah's mother shook her head. She took a deep breath and then in her usual voice she said, "I'm not angry, John. It is hard to have a child and then suddenly find he's a man, but it *is* war and our fight for independence and I understand. Go to the Town Parade, but come back tonight."

John hugged her and grinned. "You still have Hannah at home," he said. "And we will lick the Redcoats!" He shouted now. "We will drive them from Rhode Island!" He called "Good-by" and as he went out the door, he sang, "Stuck a feather in his hat and called it macaroni." Then they could hear his footsteps running, getting fainter and faster as he went down the hill and north to the Town Parade.

The song, the patriot's song, echoed in the room. Everyone knew it. It was the song the British had taunted the Americans with at first. It was the song that had now become the song of patriots and fighters.

Hannah's father and mother stood where they were when John left. Hannah was frightened at the way they looked. What could she do to make them smile, to make them move? Then she knew. John had said, "You still have Hannah at home." And it was true. She was there, ready to help.

She walked toward them then and put her hand on her mother's arm. "Mother," she said softly, "I'll help. I'll do John's work if I can."

Her mother and father looked at her as if from a great distance.

Hannah talked fast now. "I can do many things," she insisted. "I can plant. I can gather vegetables. I can milk cows. I can bring water from the well."

"Those are hard tasks, Hannah," her mother said. "You are still a child."

"I'm ten," said Hannah, "and up to now I have done only chores in the house. Polished pewter and helped to cook and knitted socks and spun and churned sometimes. But I can do other things, too. I will go and fetch the water *now*, since John forgot."

Hannah's mother smiled. "You could never bring the water back up the hill. It is so heavy."

"I can, I can," insisted Hannah. "Then I will be doing something for the war, too. Please let me try? Now? Tonight?"

Her father patted her. "Very well, try, but promise if the pails are too heavy to throw away the water and I will go and fetch it myself."

Hannah's mother nodded. "On those terms, I agree."

Hannah went just outside the door and took the

yoke and wooden pails from a bench there. She put her neck into the opening. The frame rested on her shoulders and the pails dangled from it. As she did that she suddenly had the feeling that she had put on a uniform, *her* uniform for the war. She thought, if men and boys have to leave home, then women and girls must do their work. And if the work is done, then the women and girls are helping to win the war.

She spoke through the open door. "I will call when I come back to the buttonwood tree with the water."

She walked down Green Lane, with the yoke on her shoulders and a hand on each pail that dangled from it. Then she had a thought, and she stood up even straighter and she sang softly to herself, "Stuck a feather in his hat and called it macaroni."

For, if John could sing that song on his way to enlist, then she could sing it on her way to the well to fetch the water. She sang it again, louder this time, "Yankee Doodle came to town, riding on a pony. He stuck a feather in his hat and called it macaroni."

CHAPTER TWO

"Saltpeter, Brimstone . . . and Pewter"

Hannah hummed "Yankee Doodle" all the way down the lane. The water needed tonight was for drinking and so she had to go north to the well on the other side of the Market House, for the one nearer home had salty water, good only for washing.

It pleases me, thought Hannah, that I have to go so far the first time. That will surely prove that I can do John's chores.

At the foot of the lane, near a large rock where they often sat, were several girls about Hannah's age. They were Betsy and Priscilla Goodall and Jennifer Smith, Hannah's special friend. They were playing scotch-hopper and they called to Hannah to join them.

Hannah stood a little way off and said, "I can't this evening. I must fetch water from the well."

Jennifer laughed. "Hannah," she said, "you will never carry water up that hill. Never!"

"Never. Never," chanted Betsy and Priscilla.

"I will!" Hannah shouted over their voices. "I will, I will, I will!"

Scotch-hopper seemed like a child's game to Hannah since she was now doing her brother's work. So, as she passed her friends, she scuffed through the sand, destroying the lines they had drawn for their game. The girls let out a shout and Hannah ran away as fast as she could with the pails hampering her. A pebble struck her in the back, another hit one of the pails.

Hannah ran until she was out of range of shouts and stones, then slowed down to a walk. The sun was setting and the Towne Street was bathed in a golden light. Hannah looked at the wharves and the masts lining one side of the street. She thought about the ships and the distant places they had sailed to.

Hannah's walk took her by the shops and she peered into the windows where all kinds of things were on display. One window had a bonnet in it, a pink bonnet with lace. Hannah stood and stared at it for a long time, getting as close to the glass as her pails would allow. It was a beautiful bonnet. She could have looked at it all evening, but, finally, she remembered her errand and walked on.

When she came to the Market House, she found a group of people gathered around the hay scales. Hannah knew that notices were sometimes tacked up there and so she, too, stopped, but she was too short and her pails made it impossible to get close enough to see.

No matter, she thought, I will see it on my way back.

A few yards farther and she came to the well where several people awaited their turns. They were boys, mostly, with yokes and pails like hers, but a few women and girls were there, too.

Hannah waited patiently. Then a boy about John's age said to her, "I'll fill your pails for you if

you like."

Hannah was pleased, for that was hard work. "If you want to," she said. "Thank you."

He filled them to the brim and hooked them back onto the yoke. Hannah turned to walk away, but the pails were so heavy she felt as if she were tied to the spot where she stood.

Her new friend watched her. "Too heavy?" he asked. And then he smiled slyly and added, "For a girl."

Hannah's cheeks flushed. "Girls can do this as well as boys," she retorted.

Just then there was a shout. "Hannah!"

Hannah looked. There, running across the Town Parade near the Market House, was John. She waited for him to come nearer.

He was breathless and angry. "Hannah," he said, "who told you to come here?"

Hannah became angry, too. The boy who had filled her pails was standing there, listening. "I offered," she said, "since *you* did not fetch the water."

"You can't carry it up the hill. Tell Father to fetch it."

"I will not! I said I would fetch it, and I will."

John reached for the pails. Hannah struggled, but John was stronger. He poured out some of the water. "There," he said, satisfied, "they will be lighter to carry."

Hannah glared at him. "Why aren't you enlisting?" she asked.

"It is still too early. Not enough men are here. There are some now," he said, pointing to the Parade where the soldiers drilled. "I must go. Be careful, Hannah."

Hannah tossed her head and did not answer him. Her face was scarlet with shame. Treating me like a child, she thought.

The boy who filled her pails spoke. "He doesn't think you can carry them, either."

Hannah refused to answer him. Instead, with a tremendous effort, she walked away, head high, cheeks still flushed.

But the pails were unbearably heavy; her shoulder joints seemed to stretch to the breaking point.

Somehow I will reach the Market House, she thought, and there I will rest and see what the notice says. By then I will be out of sight of this boy who thinks girls are weak.

Her anger at John and the boy seemed to give

her added strength for she managed to reach the hay scales. Again she tried to read the notice, but again she couldn't even see it because of the people.

"Please, ma'am," said Hannah to a woman standing near, "what does it say?"

The woman turned on her angrily. "It says a powder mill is to be set up in this very town to manufacture gunpowder and we shall probably all be blown out of our beds. And it says that all saltpeter and brimstone will be collected because they are necessary to make gunpowder." The woman was angry, and at the last word she stamped away.

Saltpeter and brimstone, thought Hannah—and pewter to be melted down for bullets. All the misery of the day, which had been pushed to the back of her mind by John's enlistment and the water pails, came back to Hannah. The memory of it, combined with the awful weight of the water, suddenly made her load seem heavier than before.

"I can't do it. I can't do it," she said to herself. "I will spill it out and let Father fetch it."

She tilted one pail, letting some of the water spill onto the street. And then her own words came back to her, the words about doing John's chores, and she righted the pail.

Slowly, then, inch by inch, she went a short distance down the Towne Street. Once she stumbled and almost fell. The water slopped out of the pails onto her petticoat and apron. She could feel some of it in her shoes. Hannah was altogether miserable. She sniffled, then wiped her nose on her sleeve, a thing her mother had told her never to do.

"Child!" It was her mother's voice.

Hannah took a hand off one pail and pushed her damp hair back from her forehead. She just looked at her mother and said nothing.

Her mother's voice was kind. "Father told you to throw away the water if it was too heavy," she said.

"I know," said Hannah. "So did John, so did the boy at the well, so did my friends. But I *want* to fetch it."

"I know. I know," said Mrs. Williams soothingly. "But Father has just told me there is a military display this evening in celebration of the French treaty. You have been gone a long time. If we are to see the display, we must hurry to Fox Hill. So I have come for the water. Come, take off the yoke, Hannah."

Hannah knew that voice. It was kind. It was

gentle. But underneath it was as firm as a rock. She knew there was no arguing with it. So, unwillingly, she took off the yoke and her mother carried the pails.

Hannah muttered, "I want to do my share for the war."

"You will, Hannah," her mother assured her. "You will."

Hannah raised her head. Her mother strode down the Towne Street. Hannah followed.

When they reached Green Lane it was almost dusk, but the girls were still there. They saw, at a glance, what had happened. They waited until Mrs. Williams was partway up the lane and then they called to their playmate, taunting her.

"Going to fetch the water, Hannah?"

"All the way up the hill, Hannah?"

"All by yourself, Hannah?"

Hannah could not think of an answer. She walked a little faster until she caught up to her mother. Now she was almost crying.

"What is it? What is the matter?" her mother asked.

"I remembered the pewter," said Hannah.

Her mother replied, "That is over and done

with. We are not the only ones who gave their pewter and we must not feel sorry for ourselves."

They reached the door to the house. Mrs. Williams put the pails down. "Go wash your face, Hannah, and tidy yourself and we will walk to Fox Hill."

For a moment Hannah stood facing her mother. Her face was flushed and streaked with tears. Her cap was pushed to one side. Her hair was matted with perspiration.

Her mother kissed her red-rimmed eyes. "Poor child," she murmured, and they entered the house.

Hannah's mother went to get a towel and some water. "This is not the way to begin your new life of trying to be a son and a daughter to us," she said. She set the bowl of water down near the hearth. "Come, now. Take off your apron. It is wet. Straighten your cap and comb your hair. I will bank the fire while you do that, for your father won't be home until later."

Hannah sponged her face, then climbed the stairs to her little room with the slanted ceiling and the one tiny window. It was dusk now, but she had not brought a candle. So, as best she could, she smoothed her hair and straightened her cap. She took off her rumpled apron wet with tears and with water slopped from the pails. Quickly she did all this and went back down the stairs to the kitchen.

Her mother stood at the half-open door. She spoke to her daughter without turning. "The night air is cool. You had best wear your cloak."

Dutifully Hannah took her cloak from a peg near the door. She noticed that her mother wore one, too, and carried a lantern, for it would be dark when they returned. Together she and her mother went out into the dusk.

The cool air felt as good on Hannah's face as the water had, for her cheeks and eyes were still hot.

"It will be easiest if we climb up the lane to the highway and walk toward Fox Hill," said Hannah's mother. "In that way we shall see everything."

They walked in silence up the lane past the huge rock that marked the garden, past the barn to the highway, then south to Fox Hill overlooking the harbor. The evening star hung in the sky. The air smelled sweet—a mixture of salt water and of earth newly turned for the planting.

When they reached the end of the highway,

they saw a great crowd. All the hills were covered with people who had come to see the military display. And just about then the muskets began to rattle.

Hannah's mother said into her ear, "That, I have been told, is a *feu de joie*— a fire of joy—the sound of the muskets."

Then the battery in the fort roared.

Again Hannah's mother spoke into her ear, "Count them! Thirteen cannon for thirteen states. A national salute!"

Hannah counted. And no sooner had the noise stopped echoing from the hills than a frigate in the harbor answered with its salute.

Next all faces turned to the north, for from there, from the artillery park at the college on the hill, came another *feu de joie* of muskets.

And another from a barracks where troops were quartered down in the town. From all directions, it seemed, muskets, cannon, and cheers from the townspeople gathered together.

Hannah could see that there were smiles on the faces of all the people watching.

She spoke. "How happy everyone is, Mother."

Mrs. Williams took her daughter's hand in hers.

"Yes," she said, "it is a happy occasion, for with the help of our French allies we will surely bring this war to a victorious end."

When the military display was over, Hannah and her mother started slowly back along the highway.

Hannah felt none of the joy that everyone else seemed to feel. It had been exciting, all the noise, but she was tired and could not understand everything.

Hannah's mother spoke again. She spoke almost to herself—a continuation of what she had been saying before. "It will be fine to have it all over, the war, and to return to a normal life again. It is hard for everyone."

"For Father, too?"

"Yes," Hannah's mother answered. "Your father works very hard at the foundry. That is where he went tonight. And he did want to add more rooms to the house—a parlor, some chambers—but that must wait now."

Hannah had never heard this, that the house was to be made larger. How wonderful it would be, she thought, to have a parlor and chambers and an attic and more fireplaces and fine furniture. She came naturally to the next question, "Shall we have servants then, too?"

"Perhaps," her mother said, "but that is in the future. Now there are the cannon your father makes at the furnace for the war and the Council of War he attends, and the fight for freedom."

"And the pewter to be melted down for bullets." It was as if a voice in her head said the words, not she.

"Forget about the pewter, Hannah," her mother advised.

Hannah did not answer. She could not. She knew that if she talked she would cry again. Now they picked their way down the narrow lane. Hannah's mother held the lantern so they could see the stones and ruts, and finally they came to their house. There was a glow inside.

"Father is home," said Hannah.

"Yes, he is probably very tired. We have all had an exciting day and we must go to bed early."

They opened the door. Mr. Williams sat near the hearth. His candleholder was hooked over the back of his chair. He was cleaning the gun that usually hung over the mantel. He looked up at them and smiled.

"I could hear the celebration clearly," he said. "Did you enjoy it?"

Mrs. Williams turned from hanging up the lantern and putting her cloak on a peg near the door. "Oh, yes," she said. "Did you enjoy yourself, Hannah?"

Hannah put her cloak on a peg, too. Suddenly she felt so tired . . . so tired. All she could manage to say was, "It was fine."

Her father leaned toward the fire to knock out his pipe. "Remember what you heard and saw tonight. It is a special occasion."

Hannah's mother sat down with some sewing in her hands. "Every day seems to be a special one," she answered. She turned to Hannah. "Are you hungry?" she asked.

Hannah stood in the middle of the kitchen. She felt confused. All that she had seen and heard that day raced around in her head. It had been too much. The pewter collection. John enlisting. The water pails. The well. The Town Crier. The military display. She swayed.

Her mother spoke to her gently. "Go to bed, Hannah."

Hannah kissed her mother and father and went

to the door to the stairs. She took a lighted candle from a table and went slowly up to her room.

When she was safely in bed and the candle blown out, her sleepiness vanished and she lay there in the dark, her eyes wide open, staring, thinking of the war which had suddenly come so close that it touched her and John and the house and her own pewter plate.

Just the same, she thought, one plate cannot make that much difference in the war. Not *one* plate. I must keep it. I must keep it.

A star twinkled and the curtain blew in the breeze and Hannah slept. She did not even wake when John came tramping into the house still humming "Yankee Doodle."

PART TWO *Summer, 1778*

CHAPTER THREE

"It is Hannah Williams, Sir!"

Spring grew into summer, and one warm morning early in August Hannah stood at the door to the lane tying the strings of her sunbonnet. It was so early that no one else was awake.

Hannah had been too excited to sleep any longer; she had to get up. The evening before, in the garden that she had planted and cared for all summer, she had seen several squashes which were large enough and ripe enough to pick. So she had awakened early to gather the ripe vegetables. Food was so scarce in Providence that this was the moment she had been working for all summer: to pick some of the vegetables she herself had raised from seeds and to add them to the little food they had been able to buy.

She opened the door softly and slipped out. She drew a deep breath. The air smelled of sun on dew-wet grass. Far up the hill a bird sang. In the distance, Hannah could hear the beating of a drum and the shrill note of a fife. Another company of soldiers drilling, she thought. It seemed there was always a company of soldiers drilling nowadays.

She walked a short distance up Green Lane to the large boulder that marked the entrance to the garden. Around on the other side of this rock were rows of beans and corn and squashes which she had cared for faithfully day after day since spring. And on the far side of the patch were the herbs: caraway and thyme and dill.

Hannah walked around the rock humming to herself, but then she stopped and held onto the rock for support. She felt as if she were dreaming and must hold onto something solid. The garden—

her garden—that she had tended and watched and weeded all summer was stripped! Not a squash was left, not a bean, not an ear of corn. Only torn lengths of cornstalks and squash vines.

Hannah let go of the rock. Frantically she went down the rows. She turned over every leaf, every torn vine and cornstalk.

Nothing.

Nothing was left.

In a daze she rose and brushed the soil from her hands. Then, as if coming to life, she screamed, "Mother! Mother!"

She turned and hurtled down the lane to the house. She burst into the kitchen.

"Mother," she cried, "my garden is gone!"

Her mother was just putting a kettle of water to heat on the crane in the fireplace. She almost dropped it into the fire at Hannah's entrance.

"What do you mean the garden is gone?" she asked.

"It . . . it . . ." Hannah stammered in her excitement. "There is not a squash nor an ear of corn nor a bean. Someone has taken *everything!*"

Her mother straightened up and wiped her hands on her apron. "Let me see it," she ordered.

So she and Hannah climbed back up the lane to the rock and Hannah showed her mother the torn vines, the stripped and broken cornstalks.

Her mother looked at the ruined garden for a few moments, then she put her arm around Hannah's shoulders.

"I am sorry this happened," she said, and her arm held Hannah so tightly that it hurt. "It must have been the soldiers. They are hungry and your vegetables were almost ripe."

"They *were* ripe, some of them," Hannah corrected her. "I came here early this morning so I could pick you the first squash from my garden." Now the awfulness of it came over her and she threw her apron over her face and cried.

Her mother took the apron away from Hannah's face. "You must not cry," she said in a strong voice. "This has happened to others, too. It is war. Come back to the house and eat your breakfast and we will decide what to do."

Hannah stopped crying but there was still such an ache of disappointment inside her. She had worked so hard on the garden, harder than she had to, to prove that she was grown up, that she could raise vegetables as her share of the war work. She had the feeling that her mother still thought she was a child because she had kept her pewter plate. Raising vegetables for the family would prove she was not.

And now there were no vegetables.

Hannah couldn't explain this to her mother, for since the day in spring, when the pewter collection had been made, they had never discussed it. From time to time Hannah took the plate out of her chest secretly and gloated over it. She would turn it this way and that, touch it lovingly, glad that she had kept it. Although it needed polishing, it was the only pretty thing in her life. No one knew what it meant to her to have it. And if it was childish to keep it, there were the vegetables to prove that she could be grown up, too.

Only now there were no vegetables.

Hannah's mood changed. She became angry as they went back into the house.

In the kitchen she just sat, tying and untying the strings of her bonnet, while her mother sliced bread, placed it on the toasting rack on the hearth, and mixed chocolate.

Hannah's father came in and looked around the kitchen. No one said good morning to him, no one looked at him. The atmosphere in the kitchen was tense. Hannah, who usually chatted, was quiet. Her mother looked grim.

Mr. Williams looked from one to the other. "Is something wrong?" he asked.

Mrs. Williams explained. "The soldiers have stripped Hannah's garden. Not a bean or squash or an ear of corn is left." She sounded angry now, too, for she knew how much work Hannah had put into the garden.

Her father crossed the room to Hannah. "I am sorry," he said. "I should have warned you that this might happen. Orchards and cornfields for miles around have been stripped by the hungry troops."

Hannah looked up at him. "But we are hungry, too," she said, "and there is not much to buy in the market." She stamped her foot. "I am tired of soldiers. There is nothing in Providence any longer but soldiers and marching and soldiers and marching." She took off her bonnet and threw it on the table.

Hannah's father stroked her hair. "That is true," he agreed. "The town is an armed camp, but there is reason for that. We may be attacked at any moment by the British. As for your garden, a committee already has been appointed to call on General Sullivan to complain about the soldiers trespassing on gardens and cornfields and orchards."

He sat down and drank his chocolate and ate his porridge. Hannah's mother turned the toasting rack to brown the bread on the second side, then brought the toast to the table.

They ate in silence, each busy with his own thoughts.

Then Mr. Williams rose and left the house. Hannah still sat drinking chocolate, quiet, thoughtful. Only now she was not sorrowing for the stolen vegetables, nor was she angry any longer. She was deciding on a plan.

All morning, while she helped her mother to make the beds and sweep the floors and wash the dishes, she thought of what she would do. Even while she read aloud to her mother from her primer for her usual daily reading lesson, the plan was in the back of her mind. And when her mother told her to go outdoors and play, she knew exactly where to go. *She*, Hannah Williams, would go to see General Sullivan! Why not? she thought. She would tell him what his soldiers were doing to Providence.

Hannah set off down the hill to the Towne Street. She had heard her father say that General Sullivan lived in a house on the west side of the Great Bridge. She didn't know exactly which house it was but she was sure she could find it.

As she walked down the hill, along the Towne Street, up to the Town Parade, and across the Bridge, she saw soldiers everywhere. Providence does look like an armed camp, she thought. It must be true that soon we are going to attack the British or they are going to attack us.

As she approached the western end of the bridge, there seemed to be even more soldiers, thick groups of them, standing about. They seemed to be gathering in front of a large house that faced the bridge. That house, thought Hannah, must be General Sullivan's headquarters.

Just as she had this thought, the door of the house opened and a handsome man came out. Hannah gasped. Most of the soldiers she had seen were dressed in leather breeches and homespun shirts with flintlock muskets over their shoulders. But this man sparkled and glittered. His buttons were gold and there were gold fringes on his shoulders, and his sword shone in the sun. His uniform, of buff and blue, was spotless. His white cravat seemed to gleam. Even his boots glistened. Hannah was overcome. She stopped in her tracks and stared, and then she realized that it was General Sullivan and that he was heading straight toward the bridge, toward *her!* An officer walked beside him and behind him there were soldiers as far as Hannah could see.

She became confused, then panic-stricken. She clung to the railing of the bridge. What should she do? Go back? Flatten herself against the railing? Run ahead, past the General? Hannah's knees began to shake, but before she could make up her mind what to do, General Sullivan turned to the man beside him and Hannah heard him say:

"Captain Brown, did I not tell you to clear the roads for our march? What is that child doing there? Who is she?"

His voice was gruff and angry. The Captain looked flustered.

Then Hannah was surprised to hear her own voice, thin and soft. "It is Hannah Williams, sir."

"Who?" The General was getting impatient.

Hannah was getting bolder. She stepped forward and curtsied. Louder she said, "It is Hannah

Williams, sir. I have some business with you, sir, General Sullivan."

A flicker of a smile crossed the General's face. "State your business, Hannah Williams," he ordered.

Hannah drew a deep breath, then said all at once, "I have come about my garden, sir. Your soldiers have taken all the vegetables I raised for our family because there is not enough food in Providence, and my father says your soldiers have been stripping cornfields and orchards everywhere." She ran out of breath and out of words. She stopped.

The General's face became red. He turned to Captain Brown. "Captain Brown! Is this true?"

"I am afraid so, sir."

"Did I not ask you to order the men to stop foraging for food?"

Captain Brown gulped. "You *did*, sir. And I *did*. But they still *do*."

General Sullivan's voice turned soft, but there was something in it that frightened Hannah more than his gruff voice.

"This time," said the General slowly, "you will transmit my order to all the camps hereabouts and

add that any man caught disobeying will be *severely* punished. Have my message posted in the town so that the townspeople will know it as well."

"Yes, sir," said Captain Brown. He turned on his heel and went back to headquarters.

General Sullivan smiled at Hannah. "Thank you for your information, madam. This matter will be attended to."

Hannah curtsied. Her boldness had vanished completely. She was frightened again and wanted only to get away. She muttered, "Thank you, sir," then turned and ran like the wind back across the bridge. She raced back along the way she had come, hair flying, apron flying. Only when she reached Green Lane and was part way up it did she finally slow down, then stop and look back. There below she could see the General and his troops crossing the bridge. The column of soldiers and wagons twisted and turned like a snake. Hannah's friends came from behind a house and watched with her.

Betsy said, "They are marching to Tiverton."

"How do you know?" asked Hannah.

"My father says so and he knows. From there they will cross on the ferry and drive the Redcoats from Newport!"

To Tiverton, thought Hannah. That is where John is in camp. If there is a battle, he will be fighting!

Jennifer put her arm around Hannah's waist. "We are going to pick blackberries. Come with us, Hannah."

Hannah noticed the basket Jennifer carried. Berrypicking was something Hannah loved, the prickly vines, the large black berries, but today she did not feel like picking wild berries when she couldn't pick her own vegetables. At the thought of her garden she felt tears coming to her eyes again. She turned quickly, but Jennifer saw. She saw everything.

"What is it, Hannah?" she asked. "I'm your best friend. Tell me."

"Nothing," said Hannah. "I want to go home now."

Betsy and Priscilla held their hands around her in a circle. "Come with us, Hannah," they pleaded. "You never come with us any more."

"I can't! I'm sorry, but I can't!" said Hannah, and she twisted about angrily. At last she broke away from the girls and raced up the lane, past the house to the rock. She climbed up to the flat part and sat down. There before her lay the ruined garden, with a few stalks of caraway and dill nodding in the breeze. That was all that was left of four months' hard work.

And beyond was the barn, and the fields John had plowed but never planted, for he had gone off to war. No wonder food is scarce, thought Hannah, and kicked the rock in anger, for there are no men left in the town to raise any crops.

Hannah sat thinking about General Sullivan and John and the troops and her garden until she heard her father trudging up the hill for his noontime meal. She followed him into the house.

"Well, Hannah," he said gaily, as he sat down at the table, "if you plant another garden, you will not have any trouble with the troops. General Sullivan has just sent word to our committee that his soldiers will not forage for food any longer."

"I know," said Hannah quietly.

"How do you know?" her father asked.

"I went to see him," explained Hannah, "and I told him about my garden."

"*You* went to see *General Sullivan?*" Her father sounded as if he didn't believe her, and her mother just stared at her.

"Yes, I did," said Hannah. "I met him on the Great Bridge and I told him about the squashes and the beans and he told me it would be attended to."

Mr. Williams put down the fork he had just picked up.

"Hannah," he said, "we should have appointed you a member of our committee."

Hannah's mother laughed. She looked proudly at Hannah. "Our child is growing up," she said.

Hannah blushed. She had the feeling that her mother was talking about the pewter plate when she said, "Our child is growing up."

Mrs. Williams had never mentioned the plate directly and Hannah herself had a hard place inside her which kept *her* from talking about it. The only time this feeling disappeared was when she took out the plate and looked at it. The rest of the time she tried not to think about it, for when she did the hard place came again.

She wouldn't think about it now.

She stood up. "Father," she asked, "is it too late in the summer to plant another garden?"

"You can try. If the summer is long enough and warm enough and if there is enough rain, perhaps we shall eat your beans yet."

"Then I will go and pull up what is left and start all over," said Hannah. She took her sunbonnet from a peg near the door and tied it under her chin. Then she left the house and went to her garden.

CHAPTER FOUR

"Time Will Show You How"

A few weeks later Hannah sat knitting socks near the table in the kitchen. Across from her, her mother was mending clothes. It was candlelight time. The tall candlesticks had been placed on the table and she and her mother sat close to the light. Her father would be home soon, then he would sit down and read *The Providence Gazette*, the weekly newspaper.

The tall clock ticked, the candles sputtered in the breeze. Hannah's knitting needles clicked and her mother sighed as she put down one shirt and took up another.

Hannah knew that her mother was worried about her brother John. A great battle had been fought near Newport. Reports had been brought back to Providence that many men had been killed and many more wounded, and that, in spite of all this, the British still held Newport.

Suddenly the quiet in the room was broken. Hannah's father came in and went right to the fireplace. On the wall there hung a box and from it he took his long white clay pipe. He filled it. Then, with a pair of tongs, he took an ember from the fire and lighted it. When the first cloud of smoke drifted across the room, he hung up the tongs, turned, and spoke.

"Martha," he said, talking fast, "John has been wounded."

Hannah's mother had been watching him intently. Now she dropped her sewing into her lap. Her hands were clasped together. "How badly?" she asked quietly, as if she had been expecting this news.

"He cannot be severely wounded. I don't think they would move very sick men so soon."

"Has John been moved?" Hannah's mother still spoke quietly.

"Yes, the boats carrying the wounded docked this afternoon. It was too late to go down, but I have seen a list of returned wounded. John's name is there. They have all been taken to the General Hospital on the hill."

"May we go there now? At once?" Now Hannah's mother's voice was shaking.

"I think not," answered Hannah's father. "The hospital would not want visitors tonight with so many sick and wounded to take care of. The first thing in the morning we will go, but not tonight. It is too late."

Hannah, too, had stopped knitting. John wounded, she thought, John wounded! She felt as if she were going to cry.

Her mother came over to her and pressed Hannah's head to her breast. "Don't cry, Hannah," she said in a loud voice. "Don't cry." It was as if she were telling this to herself, not to Hannah.

Hannah's father stood near. "John is probably not wounded badly," he said again soothingly, "if he has already been moved to Providence. They would not move the severely wounded men so soon. Let us bank the fire and go to bed. We will go and see him early tomorrow."

But when Hannah was in her bed, she could not sleep. She lay thinking about John wounded. She heard her mother and father talking, talking far into the night, their voices muffled by the wall. She wished she could hear what they were saying. She wondered if they knew things about John and his wound which they had not told her. Even after their voices stopped, Hannah heard the clock striking quarter hours, half hours, hours . . .

She must have slept finally, for the next thing she knew her mother was calling her from downstairs. "Hannah! Hannah! Wake up!"

Hannah woke. And remembered. John was wounded and they were going to the hospital to see him. She bounded out of bed and dressed quickly and went downstairs. Her breakfast, milk and bread, was on the table, and her mother and father were packing a basket. They put food into it, half a loaf of bread and a piece of cheese, and Hannah's mother added some linen cloths and some of John's shirts and a blanket. Hannah ate quickly, for she did not want to keep them waiting.

Soon they started out toward the college on the hill that had been turned into a hospital by the army. Everything in Providence was used by the army.

Hannah's father carried the basket and they walked together, all three. No one spoke. Hannah wanted to talk. There were so many questions she wanted to ask, but the anxious look on her mother's and father's faces kept her from saying anything.

When they reached the hospital the sun was barely over the hill, it was still so early in the day. Hannah noticed everything on the way—the bare fields, smoke rising lazily from chimneys. Down on the Towne Street she could see just the top of the church spire and high up on Prospect Hill the beacon, the tall pole with the kettle of tar ready for lighting in case the British attacked the town. Here and there the purple spikes of loosestrife bloomed along the stone walls. Providence is quiet this morning, she thought, not a company left in the town to drill.

It was so peaceful it was hard to think of a battle so nearby, but when Hannah and her mother and father went into the large brick building, they left the peaceful world and entered the world made by the war.

It was dark inside and crowded and smelled badly.

Hannah's father approached a soldier who leaned on a stick. "Do you know where I may find my son, John Williams?" he asked.

The man looked at him but did not say anything.

Hannah's father repeated his question.

"John Williams," he said, "where can I find John Williams?"

The man spoke. "I heard you the first time," he said, "but I was thinkin'. I don't know where you can find him. I never heard of him. Better ask the Ward Master."

"Where shall I find *him?*"

"Hereabouts," said the man. "Or the nurses may know."

"Thank you," said Hannah's father, and moved off. Wordlessly Hannah's mother followed and Hannah followed her.

They stopped at a door marked "Ward One." Hannah's father went in. From the door Hannah could see that the room was lined with bed sacks on which men lay. She could see bandages on heads and on hands and legs. She could hear groans, too. Her father came out.

"Not here," he said, "but one man told me where John is. The next ward, I think."

Quietly they walked to the next door. Hannah could feel her heart beating fast and hard. Would John be groaning, too?

She and her mother waited again while her father went into the room. Hannah noticed that her mother's lips were pressed together tightly. She said nothing. Hannah's father seemed to be gone a long time, but when he came out, he was smiling.

"John's here," he said, "and he's fine. Follow me."

They went just inside the door and there on a bed sack on the floor lay John. His hair fell all over the pillow, his shirt was not very clean, his right leg had a great bandage on it. He grinned.

"Mother!" he said. "Hannah!"

Hannah's mother bent and kissed him. "John," she whispered. Then again, "John!"

Hannah knew that that one word meant everything.

Hannah kneeled on the floor. She bent over, eager to speak to John, but now, like her mother, all she could say was, "John."

Hannah's mother touched John's shoulder. "Is it just your leg that's hurt?" she asked.

"Just my leg," John answered.

Hannah's father spoke. "Can you come home, do you think?"

"I think so, Father. Ask the Hospital Steward." He propped himself on his elbows. "I would like to come home. Mother could change the bandage." His voice dropped to a whisper. "I don't like it here."

Hannah looked around at the sick and wounded men. The room was noisy with talk and with clatter. There were men with splints and men who seemed to breathe hard, men who had been burned —probably by powder—men tossing with fever. There were candles here and there and stone mugs everywhere filled or half-filled with cider or with milk. The smell of the room was strong and unpleasant. No wonder John would like to come home, she thought.

They were all surprised just then to see Mrs. Smith walking toward them. She wore no cloak and she carried some splints and some bandages.

"Are you a nurse?" Hannah asked.

"I am," said Mrs. Smith.

Hannah's mother spoke quickly, urgently. "May I take my boy home?"

Mrs. Smith smiled. "You can do more for him than the surgeon here," she said. "He needs food and rest, that's all."

"But his leg . . ." said Hannah's mother.

"You can change the bandage," said Mrs. Smith. "You are as good a nurse as anyone else in Providence." She leaned over John and smoothed his hair.

"As good as anyone else," agreed John. "Or perhaps better."

"Now there. I have been reproved." Mrs. Smith was laughing.

Mr. Williams spoke. "John did not mean . . ."

"I know, I know," said Mrs. Smith. "He is a brave boy." She patted his arm. "I must go to the next ward."

They all watched her leave, and then Hannah spoke. "John," she said, "did you mind being in the battle?"

"Hush, Hannah," warned her mother, for she

didn't think that John wanted to speak of it so soon.

John turned his face to the wall and Hannah thought he would not answer her question, but then he looked directly at them all. "I did not mind the battle," he explained, and his face became flushed. "I fought as well as anyone, I'll wager. With my bayonet . . . I fought a Hessian with just my bayonet! Only we had to fight all day with nothing to eat and my friend was killed and the sound of the bombardment kept on and on and it rained and all our ammunition was wet. We lay under the fences, waiting, waiting for the Redcoats to come, and there were no bullets to use, only our bayonets." His voice rose in excitement. "And, Father, the British call us traitors. Do you know that?"

"I know," said Hannah's father, and Hannah noticed his hands were clenched and the knuckles were white.

"Traitors!" said John, and his eyes flashed. "When we fight to be a country, the thirteen United Colonies! If only the powder hadn't been wet! If only . . ." His voice became so low they all leaned forward to hear. "And then in the night

we retreated to Tiverton and the British still hold Newport." He turned to Hannah. "No, Hannah, I did not mind being in the battle, but I wish that we had won it."

Hannah's mother smoothed the hair back from John's forehead. "You have done your share, John. Now rest. Father will come in a carriage for you after dinner. He will speak to the Hospital Steward now." She left the basket near the sack on which he lay. She stood upright and spoke to Hannah's father, "Richard, you will attend to everything?"

"Yes, Martha, you and Hannah go home now. I will attend to everything."

Shyly Hannah patted John's hand. "Good-by, John," she said. "I am glad you are to be home again."

John laughed and said, "I am glad, too!"

Hannah and her mother walked out of the room and so out of the hospital, out of hearing of the groans of the wounded men, and out of sight of their feverish faces and bandaged arms and legs.

They did not speak. They walked slowly toward the lane and home.

But inside Hannah something trembled to be

said. Something seemed to choke her.

She swallowed hard and then she said, "Mother?"

"Yes, child?"

Hannah swallowed again. "Mother, I . . . I . . . am not happy any more about keeping the pewter plate."

For almost six months she had not wanted to talk about it. Now she felt she had to. The hard place was gone and she was able to speak now.

She went on. "I . . . I . . . have looked at it sometimes and I was always glad that I kept it. You never spoke to me about keeping it."

"There was nothing to say, Hannah. It was your plate to do with as you wished. I knew you were not altogether happy about keeping it."

"I thought I was," said Hannah, "but when I thought of it I seemed to get a hard place in here." She pointed to her chest. "Although I was glad to have it, I had this feeling and that kept me from talking to you about it."

"I know," said Hannah's mother, and reached over and took Hannah's hand in hers. "And now you want to talk about it?"

"It is because I have seen John," answered Hannah. "If I had given my plate there would have been a few more bullets and perhaps it would have helped."

"Perhaps it would," agreed Hannah's mother, "but you must not blame yourself. John is all right now, his leg will get better."

"Yes, I know that," said Hannah, "but I feel . . . I feel as if I had done something bad." She stopped and looked up at her mother, pleading. Her eyes were wet and her cheeks flushed. "How shall I make up for it, Mother? I must make up for it. How shall I?"

Hannah's mother thought for a minute and then she said, "Time will show you how, child. I cannot tell you. Time will show you how."

It seemed to Hannah that the hard place inside her was now both hard and heavy.

She tried to take a deep breath past the feeling in her chest, but she could not.

How childish I was, she thought, to keep a pewter plate—a small pewter plate—when we are fighting for such a big thing: as John said, to be a country!

CHAPTER FIVE

"My Days Have Been so Wondrous Free"

The days and weeks passed slowly, but each day Hannah could see that John's leg was healing.

Now, the winter's first snow was falling. It was Sunday. When Hannah awoke, it was strangely still. Every sound was muffled by the snow. In spite of the war, in spite of the hard times, Hannah was suddenly filled with excitement. She had always become excited when the first snow of the season fell. Now she stood in front of the window while she dressed, shivering in the cold and watching the snow settle on her window sill and on the barn roof. Snow, she thought, is so beautiful!

Not only outdoors, but inside the house, too, it seemed unusually quiet. Hannah was sure she must be the first to be up and about. She tiptoed down the stairs and across the kitchen to the door, for she had decided to go outdoors to feel the snow. The fire burned brightly and the kettle on the crane boiled, but there was no one in the kitchen. Hannah took a cloak from a peg on the wall, opened the door, stepped out, and closed the door softly behind her. She clutched the cloak close, for it was cold. She lifted her face and felt the snowflakes fall gently but with a little sting on her cheeks. Just then a ball of snow hit her in the face. The impact was so strong that it almost knocked her over. Her cheeks burned and hurt. She heard a laugh, and then she saw her brother John come out from behind the buttonwood tree. He limped toward her, grinning.

"Like snow, Hannah?" he asked, fingering a snowball.

"I love snow!" Hannah retorted. She reached down and gathered some in her hands. Quickly she formed a snowball, aimed, and threw it at John. It hit him in the stomach.

He laughed again. "Oh, so you want to fight?" He limped toward her and grabbed her.

She struggled, but he was stronger and bigger than she. He took snow and rubbed her face with it until her cheeks flamed and there was a blue look around her nose.

"Enough?" he kept asking. "Enough?"

Hannah shook her head stubbornly. She didn't mind the feel of the snow on her face. What she minded was that John was getting the better of her. She struggled with all her might and finally tore loose from his grip. Now she didn't bother to make a snowball. She simply scooped snow over John. Wilder and wilder the fun became. Hannah and John were both laughing loudly and rolling in a snowbank. Hannah felt so free. It was the way it used to be when she was a child. Snow. And laughter. And John playing with her.

In the midst of the wildest shriek of laughter

Hannah heard her mother's voice loud and stern. "Hannah! John! Stop that this minute. Do you hear me?"

And then she was standing over them saying, "Get up, Hannah. This is Sunday. I never heard such a noise on a Sunday. John, I'm ashamed of you! Get up!"

Hannah jumped up quickly and stood brushing off her clothes which were caked with snow. John got up, too.

"I'm sorry," he said. "I didn't think about it being Sunday."

"Nor I," said Hannah. "I was so excited by the snow, Mother."

Hannah's mother's stern look relaxed. "Come indoors now," she said.

They went inside and stood awkwardly, not knowing what to do. Neither Hannah nor John had anything to say. Hannah's mother looked as if she would say a great deal, but then a softness came over her face. "It is the first snow of the year, that is true," she said, "but it is also the Sabbath. Go upstairs and change your clothes, Hannah. John, I'm surprised you didn't hurt your leg. Hurry, now, both of you put on dry things. Hannah, be quick, it is almost time to leave for church."

Meekly Hannah ran up the stairs and quickly changed to dry clothes. She picked up her best bonnet as her mother's voice came floating up to her. "Are you almost ready?"

Hannah tied the ribbons under her chin as she came down the stairs. "Here I am," she said.

"Put on your clogs," her mother ordered.

So Hannah took them out of the cupboard—thick pieces of wood lifted from the ground on a circle of iron, with straps to go over her shoes. Her mother wore them, too, for the soles of their shoes were made of paper and the clogs would help to keep their feet dry.

"We must hurry or we'll be late," Hannah's mother urged.

Hannah turned to John. "You are not coming?"

"Mother and I decided that I had better not walk all that way in the snow even though my leg is much better."

Hannah's mother added, "It may be icy later on. I wouldn't want John to hurt his leg again when it is healing so well."

"Then only you and I are going?" asked Hannah.

"Only the womenfolk will be there," agreed Hannah's mother. "Your father cannot observe

Sunday if the Redcoats do not. Cannon must be cast on Sunday as on all the other days during a war."

John spoke defensively. "*All* the foundries and blacksmith shops and powder mills keep working. It is not only Father."

"I do not blame your father, John," answered Hannah's mother quickly. "It is the way of life in wartime. But I feel that everything should stop on Sunday so that everyone can attend church. It would be better for all concerned to pray to God than to shoot off their cannon today." She put on her bonnet and her cloak. "Come, Hannah," she said.

John limped to the door and opened it and Hannah and her mother went out into the lane.

When John had closed the door behind them, they were left alone in the snow-white world. Not only was everything around them white, but the very air was white, too, filled with snowflakes.

Hannah watched them land on her cloak. Pretty white stars. If only they wouldn't melt.

Hannah's mother took her arm. "Isn't it beautiful?" she asked. "It covers all the scars."

"What scars?" asked Hannah, thinking of the

large red scar on John's leg.

"The scars we humans make on the earth," said her mother. "The houses we build and the wells we dig and the broken fences we never mend."

Hannah turned this over in her mind for a while and then she said, "But all those things must be that way, mustn't they, Mother?"

Her mother sighed. "Of course," she said. "I'm sorry, Hannah, I did not mean to sound discouraged, but . . ." Her voice trailed off.

Hannah looked at her mother. Against the white snowflakes she seemed to see her mother's face clearer than usual, and Hannah noticed that two deep lines had formed on either side of her nose and mouth and she looked tired.

Quickly Hannah asked, "Are you all right, Mother?"

Her mother looked at her. "Yes, child. Only tired. So tired. And so worried about your aunt Abigail in Newport. So many ships of truce have gone over to bring out the inhabitants. Providence is filled with refugees from Newport, but she has not come. I don't understand why."

Hannah knew nothing to say to make her mother feel better so she only pressed her mother's hand where it lay on her arm.

And so they walked along. Now there were footprints in the snow, for there were people walking ahead of them, all going to church. Time and again Hannah and her mother said, "Good morning" to friends and neighbors.

It is pleasant, thought Hannah, to be walking to church in the snow with the church bell ringing so clear.

Clearer and louder it sounded as they approached the church, calling, calling for all to come and worship.

In the vestibule of the church there was much talk and stamping of feet. Hannah heard of the new scare—that Providence might be attacked at any moment by the British. She also heard of the rumor that many pillagers were about—soldiers from Newport who would steal anything.

On one side of the vestibule stood a group of people Hannah had never seen before.

"Who are they?" Hannah asked her mother in a whisper.

"Refugees from Newport."

Hannah passed into the church and looked at these people pityingly, for they no longer had any homes.

At last everyone was seated and the service began. Hannah could not hear the minister at first, for there was a rustling all over the church as people settled down. Then, when it was quiet, Hannah realized for the first time how cold her feet were. Neither she nor her mother had remembered to bring a foot stove. Hannah twisted and tugged at her skirts, hoping to pull them close around her shoes, and she must have made some noise, for her mother looked at her warningly.

Hannah froze to attention; she did not want her mother to have to quiet her like a child.

She decided to take her mind off her cold feet by counting the bonnets with feathers on them that she could see without turning her head. This was a favorite game of Hannah's in church. Sometimes she counted hoods or hats instead, sometimes she counted cloaks, sometimes coats.

She had counted five bonnets with feathers when suddenly the minister's voice sounded louder than usual, as if he were in the next seat.

". . . the highest and most satisfactory achievement of man can only come through sacrifice," he said.

Hannah moved as if a pin had pricked her. The words "through sacrifice" seemed to be particularly loud and clear. "Through sacrifice." But she had not sacrificed anything, she thought. She had not given her pewter plate. She had kept it.

Again the minister's voice sounded as if he stood at her elbow. "Ease and pleasure on every side to tempt the soul, but God summons it to victory through suffering."

Hannah squirmed.

Her mother whispered, "Be quiet, child."

Hannah sat up straight and held her breath. Her heart pounded. The minister was talking to her. That was it. He was talking to *her!*

In a voice of thunder he said, "To every sorrowful experience that is faithfully endured, He has added a glorious reward. All life is a trust, all gifts a trust, all opportunity a trust; faithfulness bringing blessing; uselessness bringing penalty."

Hannah began to tremble. Could he know about the pewter plate?

His voice rolled on. "For unto whomsoever much is given, of him much shall be required." He leaned forward and stretched out his arm to its full length with a long finger pointing.

He's pointing at me, Hannah thought wildly. Oh, why didn't I give my pewter plate? Why did

I keep it? Why?

The word *why* shrieked in Hannah's mind and was echoed by the minister: "Why?" he asked, "why has this war not been won? Because of your sins."

Hannah couldn't bear to hear another word. He knew, he knew about the plate. He was talking directly to her. She moaned and her mother, noticing how pale she looked, asked, "Hannah, are you sick?"

Somehow Hannah managed to shake her head. "No," she said. "Cold, so cold."

Her mother put an arm around her and held her close. Hannah shivered, but it was not only the cold. It was fear—fear of the minister's next words and fear of what she had done. She buried one ear in her mother's shoulder and pulled her cloak up around the other so she wouldn't hear any more. That way she remained for the rest of the sermon.

Gradually her shivering stopped and she grew warmer, but the words seemed to burn into her brain: "Why has this war not been won? Because of your sins."

Oh, thought Hannah, if I could only go back to last spring! I would give my pewter plate to be melted down for a bullet.

But time cannot be turned back. It was not spring, it was the end of a service on a Sunday in winter.

Hannah and her mother did not stop to exchange greetings with anyone, but hurried out of the church. When they reached the street they found that the snow had stopped, but it was colder than it had been earlier in the morning.

Hannah hugged herself inside her cloak. She could feel her mother's eyes on her, but she refused to meet their glance.

After they had walked part of the way home Hannah's mother said, "Were you feeling sick in church, Hannah?"

Hannah shook her head. "No, Mother."

"You were restless and shivering."

"It was so cold," said Hannah. But this was only half the truth.

Her mother reached out and felt Hannah's face. "Now your cheeks are flaming. Your face is hot."

Hannah finally looked at her mother. "I don't feel sick," she said, and with that they stopped talking until they reached home.

When dinner was ready, Hannah sat down at the table, with everyone else, but she was not hungry. Twice she was about to lay down her knife and fork, but she felt her mother's eyes on her and so she continued to chew and swallow as best she could.

John and her father and mother talked a great deal, but Hannah was quiet. She could think of nothing to say. Your sins, she kept thinking, because of your sins.

How the afternoon and evening passed that Sunday Hannah never remembered, but somehow they did, and early in the evening she took a lighted candle and went upstairs to her room.

She placed the candle on a table. She opened the chest and as she did so a thought came to her—to look at the pewter plate. She had not looked at it since the day John came home from the hospital, but now she wanted to see it. She reached under the clothes in the chest. Her hand struck it and she pulled it out. Amazed, Hannah looked at it. It had turned black, from not being polished.

Black as sin, thought Hannah, and she dropped

the plate back into the chest and slammed down the lid. She ran from the room, down the stairs, to the kitchen.

As she appeared in the doorway, her mother started up from her chair by the fire and came toward her.

"Hannah," she said, alarmed, "what is it? You look as if you have seen a ghost."

Hannah tried to talk, but no words came.

Her mother folded her in her arms. "Hannah, Hannah! Child, what is the matter? You have acted strangely all day. Come to bed."

At last Hannah spoke. "No!" she shouted. "Not to bed!"

"Why not?" asked her mother patiently. "I'll go with you. I'll fetch another quilt. Come along." And half-carrying Hannah, who protested all the way, she led her up the stairs to her room.

By then Hannah was crying as well as shaking. Gently her mother put her into her bed and from John's room across the hall brought another quilt. She tucked Hannah in and then sat near, stroking her hair and patting her hand.

Hannah tried to stop shaking; she clenched her teeth and tried. But she couldn't control the tears.

They ran down her cheeks and moistened the pillow.

All this time Hannah's mother didn't say a word, only stroked Hannah's forehead and smiled reassuringly and looked at Hannah lovingly with her kind eyes. For a long time they stayed that way until the shaking stopped and soon the tears. At last Hannah lay quiet, staring at the flickering candle.

Then Hannah's mother began to sing softly, a song Hannah had not heard since she was a little child.

"My days have been so wondrous free.
The little birds that fly
With careless ease from tree to tree
Were but as blest as I."

How long ago that was, she thought, when my days were wondrous free.

Hannah's mother asked, "Do you remember that song, Hannah?"

Hannah nodded to show that she did.

"It was when you slept in your trundle bed that I used to sing it to you."

Hannah remembered the low bed that was

pushed under her mother's and father's large one in the daytime and pulled out at night.

Her mother was speaking. "Hannah, my dear," she said gently, "if something troubles you, you must tell me. Are you sick?"

"No," said Hannah, "I am not sick." She paused, and then in a flood the words came. "It's only that . . . it is the pewter plate again. I think about it all the time, I cannot stop thinking about it. It was wrong of me to keep it and today the minister pointed at me in church."

Hannah's mother stirred and started to speak, but Hannah wouldn't let her. She sat up in bed.

"He did," she repeated. "He pointed at *me* when he said that our sins kept us from winning the war. And when I came up here to my room tonight I looked at the plate. I haven't looked at it since John came home. It has turned black! I'm afraid, Mother, I'm afraid!"

Hannah buried her face in her mother's breast. Her mother held her close and kissed the top of her head. "There is nothing to be afraid of, Hannah," she said reassuringly. "You are growing up. You have a conscience."

"Conscience?" asked Hannah, lifting her head.

"Yes, conscience. You are beginning to feel the difference between the goodness or badness of the way you act and you know you must do right and be good. We talked about this the day we first saw John and you asked me then how to make up for keeping the plate and I told you time would show you how. And so it will. Your conscience was stirring then. Now it is awake. That is what made you think the minister pointed at you."

"He did," Hannah said again.

Her mother shook her head. "No," she said, "he did not. He pointed at all of us. The sermon was for all of us. There is not one person in all the world who has not sinned somehow and who cannot repent and atone for his sin. You must not let it upset you so, Hannah. Everything will come out all right. You *must* go to sleep now. I will stay here until you do."

She pushed Hannah down onto her pillow and tucked in the quilt.

Then softly she began to sing again.

Hannah lay quietly, thinking over what her mother had said. Finally she sighed, a deep, deep sigh. She turned on her pillow and rubbed her cheek lovingly against her mother's hand.

I will not be afraid, she thought, while Mother sits there and sings. And somehow I will make up for keeping the pewter plate. Soon, soon I will make up for it. Soon. Soon.

She closed her eyes at last and over her there fell gently, like a warm, soft blanket, the beautiful sound of her mother's voice:

"My days have been so wondrous free.
The little birds that fly
With careless ease from tree to tree
Were but as blest as I."

Hannah slept.

CHAPTER SIX

"Porter . . . John Porter"

The next morning Hannah awoke with a start. John stood near her bed shaking her and shouting, "Hannah! Hannah! Wake up!"

Hannah's head felt as if it would snap off with each shake. She pushed John's hands away and sat up in bed. She felt confused. Something was the matter. She tried to think what it was, but before she could decide, John said in an excited voice:

"The fire bell! Hannah, the fire bell!"

The fire bell, thought Hannah. That's what makes the air shake with excitement. Now she could hear it clanging, clanging, telling all to come and help.

"You'll have to take our fire buckets," said John. "Father's gone to the foundry and Mother's nursing at the hospital. You'll have to help. *I* can't run. Get up, Hannah, quick. Quick! Get up!"

Hannah threw back the quilts. "Yes, John," she said. "Fetch the fire buckets while I dress."

John left to pick up the two leather buckets which everyone in the town kept on hand in case of fire while Hannah somehow got into her clothes. She jammed a cap onto her uncombed hair and ran downstairs. She snatched a cloak from the pegs by the door. She took the fire buckets John held out to her, one in each hand.

"Which way shall I go, John?" she asked, pausing for a moment on the doorstep.

"Mr. Smith just ran toward the Towne Street. You'll be able to tell when you reach the bottom of the hill and see the crowd. Oh, run, Hannah! I wish *I* could. Run!"

Hannah ran, in the bitter cold of the early morning. She ran as fast as she could down the hill to the Towne Street, for she knew that if *their* house were on fire, everyone in the town would come with buckets and help to put the fire out.

As Hannah turned into the Towne Street she saw a great many boys and men running north, toward the Market House and the Church. All of them carried buckets, empty, of course. Once they got to the fire they would form a line from the river to the burning building. They would pass the filled buckets up and the empty buckets down.

Hannah looked at the people, all with their faces strained, running as fast as they could. She fell in behind them. Only men and boys, she thought, and then, proudly, I am the only girl with fire buckets.

She increased her speed until she caught up to a boy about her own age. "Where is the fire?" she shouted.

He turned his head toward her. "Don't know," he said, and ran even faster. Hannah could see that his face was wet with sweat although the day was cold.

Hannah's heart beat fast with the running and with excitement and then, suddenly, before the crowd reached the Market House, there was a glare against the sky, a loud explosion, and then dense smoke rising from the north part of town.

The people around Hannah slowed down, hesitated. There was a look of terror on their faces. Some stopped and milled about, but Hannah ran on until she caught up with a large group of men, then stopped and listened to them.

"It must be the powder mill," said one.

"What else lies over there?" asked another.

"What else would cause an explosion like that—a red glare and then dense smoke?" It was the first man speaking again.

"Of course it is the powder mill," agreed a third man.

Powder mill, thought Hannah, and she felt frightened. An explosion in the powder mill! That's where they made the ammunition for the soldiers!

Afraid, she wandered from group to group listening to the discussion, uncertain, just as the others were, whether to go on or to go home.

As the townspeople stood in groups debating about the explosion, wondering what to do, a man on horseback appeared. He rode fast, and as he passed them he called out:

"Powder mill demolished! Return to your homes! Powder mill demolished! Return to your homes!"

"What next?" asked a man, standing near Hannah. "Oh, Lord, what next?"

"Excuse me," Hannah said to him, "what does demolished mean?"

"It means," explained the man, and he spoke slowly and carefully, "it means it has been blown to bits with everything and everyone in it."

"Oh," said Hannah, understanding now, "then we cannot help?"

"No," said the man sadly, "we cannot help. We do not have to go any farther."

Hannah looked around. People were turning and going back the way they had come and so, still uncertain, she turned, too.

She realized then that all was quiet, the bell had stopped clanging. She started homeward slowly, swinging the leather buckets which she had not needed. I didn't help after all, she thought. Nobody helped.

She looked behind her. To the north there was now only a thin plume of smoke in the sky.

Hannah was disappointed because she hadn't

helped. She was frightened by the explosion. She was cold.

She shivered. After the exertion of running she felt the cold strike right through the cloak and her dress.

As she turned from the Towne Street into Green Lane, a voice said to her, "Where was the fire?"

Hannah looked to one side and there, sitting on the rock where she and her friends often sat, was a young man with short black curly hair and black eyes. He wore a light gray coat that was very ragged. His shoes and breeches were ragged, too. He sat with his hands on a stick and his chin on his hands. It seemed odd to Hannah that he just sat there while all the excitement was taking place so near.

He spoke again. "Where was the fire?" He looked at her closely.

"There was no fire," answered Hannah slowly, "only an explosion in the powder mill." And then she asked the question that was in her mind. "Why did you not run with everyone else?"

"I cannot run any more," he said. "Do you have a powder mill here in Providence?"

"We did have," said Hannah, "until just now."

Then, since he didn't seem to know Providence, she asked, "You do not live here?"

"No."

"And why can't you run?" This still bothered Hannah.

He lifted his stick in one hand and tapped his leg gently with it.

Oh, thought Hannah. A wounded soldier. Another thought popped into her head. He looks like a refugee from Newport.

She asked him, "Are you from Newport?"

He nodded.

Hannah walked closer and stood in front of him. "Then you do not have a home any longer?" she asked.

He shook his head. This time it meant *no*.

Hannah's heart gave a great thump. Here, here was a way to make up for the pewter plate!

Aloud she said quickly, "If you would like to have a place to sleep I can fix one for you in our barn." Then because that invitation had not sounded exactly right, she explained, "I would offer you a place in our house, but it is so small. My father intends to add many rooms to it after the war. And my brother fought near Newport and

RW

was wounded and he is at home again. That is why I cannot offer you his bed."

The young man stood up. "I was wounded in the same battle," he said. Then he added, "I accept your offer of a place in the barn."

Hannah smiled. "Oh," she said, "my brother John and I will make it comfortable for you."

Hannah was filled with joy. From top to toe she glowed with happiness. She was so glad to be helping someone, somehow. She talked all the way up the hill.

"Did you know my aunt in Newport?" she asked. "Aunt Abigail Greene?"

The young man shook his head. "No," he said, "I did not know your aunt."

Hannah was disappointed for a moment for it would have been pleasant to take some news of her aunt to her mother. But then she became talkative again. "How was your leg wounded?" she asked and, without waiting for an answer, she went on, "You and my brother will have a great deal to talk about."

The young man stopped and looked at Hannah sternly. "I will not talk about it."

Hannah was surprised, but then she remembered

that John had not enjoyed talking about the battle at first, either.

"You do not have to if you don't want to," she assured him.

By that time, although they walked slowly because of the young man's wounded leg, they reached the buttonwood tree.

"Wait here," said Hannah. "I will go and tell my brother that I found you."

She walked up to the door, returning the fire buckets to the place on one side where they were usually kept. John threw open the door.

"Why are you back so soon?" he asked.

"The powder mill is blown to bits."

John was eager. "What happened? Tell me what happened?"

"We didn't have to go all the way to the mill," said Hannah impatiently. "John, listen . . ."

But John interrupted, "I am listening. What happened at the mill?"

"I don't know what happened." Hannah didn't want to discuss the explosion. Her mind was now set on one thing: to give the man a place to sleep. "I found a refugee from Newport and I told him he could sleep in the barn."

"Barn?" repeated John. "It's winter, Hannah. He'll freeze."

"We can make him comfortable there, John. I told him he could sleep there. I *have* to help him."

"Why?" John took up a knife and began to whittle a piece of wood.

For some reason this infuriated Hannah.

"Because nothing I do for the war comes out right," she said loudly, and her voice choked and tears stood in her eyes. "I tried to fetch water when you enlisted and it was too heavy. After the first time they wouldn't let me do it again. I planted a garden so that I could have some food to give Mother and Father and the soldiers stole everything. Just now I was the only girl with fire buckets on the Towne Street, but there was no fire. I *must* do something for this soldier." Her voice was tense and excited. "John, will you help me? Will you?" she begged.

John looked at Hannah. He had never seen her so serious. Her face was flushed; she looked desperate. He put down his knife and the stick.

"I'll help," said John. "If it means so much to you. Where is he?"

Hannah let go of the table which she had been

clinging to. Relief flooded her face. "He's near the buttonwood tree."

She and John walked down the short path to the buttonwood tree where the young man stood.

Hannah introduced them. "This is my brother John," she said.

John put out his hand. This seemed to be the last thing the young man expected; there was such a startled look on his face. Finally he put out his hand, too. He stammered, "It was good of your sister to offer to help me but I don't know now if I should accept her offer."

"We'll arrange it somehow," said John. "What is your name?"

The young man stammered again, then he smiled and said, "The same as yours. John."

"Oh," said Hannah, "imagine! But what is your last name? Ours is Williams. John and Hannah Williams. What are you called? John what?"

There was a pause. Hannah thought, he must be frightened of John. He did not stammer so much with me.

"Porter," said the young man at last. "My name is John Porter."

Hannah's brother interrupted. "Well, come and

have some breakfast. Hannah, you must be hungry."

"I could eat a roasted ox," said Hannah, "but a cup of chocolate will be most welcome."

"Mother fixed some before she left for the hospital."

"Hospital?" asked the young man. "What does she do at the hospital?"

"She is going to nurse the sick and wounded," said John, "but she is only beginning today."

"Only today?"

Hannah quickly defended her mother. She was angry at his question. "She has been nursing John at home," she explained, "and now that his leg is better, she is going to nurse the other wounded men."

The young man smiled and said, "I meant no insult to your mother."

There was an awkward pause. Then Hannah thought, *We* asked questions, he can, too. She smiled at him.

John went into the house. "Come along," he called back. "Breakfast is ready."

Hannah and the young man followed John inside. The kitchen was warm, with a roaring fire burning in the fireplace. John quickly took a loaf of bread and started to slice it. There was some cheese on the table. The kettle was boiling and soon they were all drinking hot chocolate and eating bread and cheese. John talked about the explosion at the powder mill. He wondered what had caused it. All the time Hannah and the young man ate, John talked and talked about soldiers, about fighting, about ammunition, about the explosion.

Hannah ate hurriedly, for she was very hungry, but the young man must have been starving, for he ate even faster than she did. He ate like someone who has not seen any food for a long, long time.

After they had finished eating, Hannah started to wash the dishes while the two boys went out to look at the barn.

As they walked down the path, Hannah called John back to the door. She spoke in a low voice so that only he would hear. "Please, John," she said, "be careful. He was wounded in the same battle as you, but he doesn't want to speak of it."

"All right," John said agreeably, "I understand how that is. I won't talk about it."

"And," added Hannah, "we have dozens of quilts and blankets so he can be made warm if you can find enough hay left to make a bed."

"I'll arrange something," promised John. "Don't worry, Hannah."

"I want to help him," Hannah whispered tensely. "He's a refugee from Newport and I want him to be comfortable. This is my chance to do something to help the war!"

"All right," said John, and limped away.

Hannah watched from the door. John and the young man were about the same height, but one was dark and one was fair. Both limped. Both wounded in the same battle, thought Hannah. And both called John!

Hannah felt that she loved this young man already—in these few minutes—nearly as much as her brother John. Yes, nearly, she said to herself, and then she thought, or more perhaps. For John needed no one, but the young man needed her to help him. Hannah was glad that he needed her.

She turned from the door singing. And inside her there was no longer a place heavy with guilt. Her heart was so light with joy that it sang, too.

PART FOUR *Spring, 1779*

CHAPTER SEVEN

". . . by the Rules of Martial Law"

Hannah wanted to do many things to help John Porter, but she could do none of them, for as soon as he moved into the barn he told them that he was going to work for a blacksmith on the other side of the river. There, he said, he would take his meals and would come to the barn only at night, because the blacksmith had no place for him to sleep.

But, while Hannah hardly ever talked with him,

she sometimes saw him coming and going. Often she looked at his lantern light in the barn from the window in her room and she felt happy, knowing she had found him a place to sleep.

Toward spring, when the snow began to melt and the weather turned warmer, many of the soldiers in the hospital went back to their farms. Then Hannah's mother, who had been nursing them, stayed at home sometimes. On those days Hannah was allowed to do what she wanted to.

On such a day, a mild day early in the spring, Hannah was excused from all household duties so that she could go to the Town Parade and watch the soldiers drill. It was a special day because John was to drill for the first time since he had re-enlisted in the Continental Army. Besides, Baron Steuben, the Inspector-General of the Army, had come to Providence to review the troops.

Hannah felt gay as she started off down the lane. The sun was warm on her back and she remembered the day just like this one the year before when John had enlisted for the first time.

How long ago, Hannah thought, how long ago that seemed!

As Hannah came nearer to the Town Parade,

she heard fifes and drums and the murmuring and shouting of a crowd of people. When she saw how large the crowd was, it seemed to her that everyone in the town must have come to see the review.

Hannah pushed her way through and stood at the edge of the parade ground. On the opposite side, just forming, was John's company. Hannah looked for her brother, and when she spied him, she thought proudly, How nice he looks! He doesn't even limp any more.

Hannah searched the crowd for her friends.

As she looked around, her eye was caught by two young men crouching over near the wall of the Market House. They were in the shadow of the building, but Hannah could see that one was a soldier holding a gun and the other—why, the other was John Porter!

Hannah became excited. Is today a holiday for everyone? she wondered. John Porter is not working, either.

She tried to get over to him, but the crowd had become so dense that she could not push through. She wanted to reach him since she could not find her friends. She wanted to watch the review with someone. I will go around the Market House and reach him from the other side, she decided. And so she did.

As she turned the corner of the building, he was still there, but he and the soldier paid no attention to Hannah. When she came nearer, John Porter did not even look up, he was so intent on what he was saying. Then Hannah saw the soldier hand his gun to John Porter. John looked at it carefully and put it down beside him. Quickly he took a purse from his pocket, counted out some coins, and gave them to the soldier. The man leaped to his feet with the money in his hand and ran off. Smiling after him, John Porter stood against the building and slid the gun behind his back.

Hannah was astonished by what she had seen. John Porter had bought a gun from a soldier. That was against the law! Why, only last Saturday her father had read aloud to them a long piece about it from *The Providence Gazette*. Hannah remembered how he had slapped the paper down on the table and had said, "It is time they made a law against it!"

Then another thought came to Hannah. Perhaps John Porter didn't know about the law. She went up to him.

"Hello," she said, and smiled.

He looked startled. "Oh, Hannah," he said, "what are you doing here?"

"I came to see Baron Steuben review the troops. And John is drilling today, too!"

"More fool he!" said John Porter.

Hannah was surprised. "Why do you say that?" she asked.

John Porter mumbled. "It's a lost cause, that's why."

Hannah became angry. "But John *wants* to fight for his country!"

John Porter shifted his weight from one foot to the other. He chewed his lip and said nothing.

"You have a gun," said Hannah. "Why did you buy it from a soldier?"

"Why not?" asked John Porter. "They have enough of them."

"No, they do not." Hannah's voice was loud. "They do not have enough of them. And, besides, there is a law against buying them from soldiers."

"I didn't know that." His voice turned soft. "I didn't know that," he repeated.

Just then the drums began to roll again and the

fifes to shrill, and the troops marched across the Town Parade. Hannah and John Porter watched.

On the other side of the parade ground Baron Steuben watched, too.

When the soldiers finally halted and drew up for inspection, John Porter moved a little away from Hannah. She followed quickly, she didn't quite know why.

"I, too, am tired of the review," she said; then added, "Where are you going now?"

"To the barn."

"Is today a holiday for you?" Hannah tried to think of something to talk about for she was anxious to stay with him.

"Yes, a sort of holiday." Hannah had the feeling that he carried the gun as if he didn't want anyone to see it. But he couldn't hide it, for a musket is a hard thing to hide.

Hannah looked at it again. It looked brand new.

She looked at John Porter again, too. She had not seen him close like this in a long time. He would not meet her glance. He seemed to look everywhere but at her. Whatever is the matter with him? Hannah thought. She stopped talking since he wouldn't answer.

In silence they walked the rest of the way along the Towne Street.

When they reached the lane she said, "I will show you *The Providence Gazette* for last Saturday that tells about buying things from soldiers."

"I will be happy to see it," he answered.

With that they walked in silence until they reached the house.

In the front room Hannah took the newspaper from the mantel and spread it out on the table. She bent over it. "Here it is," she said, marking the place with her forefinger.

John Porter stood near the door. "You read it," he said.

Hannah picked up the newspaper and read:

> " 'Those persons who have purchased ammunition, clothing, blankets or military stores from the soldiers in this department, are hereby directed to deliver in the same at headquarters immediately. And the General takes this method to give notice that such neglect to bring in such articles as they have purchased from the soldiers and all persons who may in future purchase such articles from them shall

be considered as interfering with the policy and safety of the army and be proceeded against by the rules of martial law.' "

Hannah finished and looked at him. "You see," she said. "I was right."

"Yes," he said. "You were right about the newspaper."

"Will you turn the gun in to headquarters then?"

"No! I will not." He looked at Hannah boldly. "I need the gun. I shall keep it. I am sorry I broke a law, but I did not know about it. I shall keep the gun." He walked up to Hannah. His face suddenly looked queer and there was a threat in his voice. "And I don't think, if I were you, I would tell anybody."

Hannah felt frightened. "Why should I tell? I will not tell," she promised.

With that he turned abruptly, opened the door, and went out. Hannah watched him go. She noticed that, like John, he did not limp any more.

It crossed her mind that he had not limped for a long, long time. It crossed her mind, too, that

PROVIDENCE
NOTICE

he did not seem so nice today as he had the day she brought him home. And she wondered why he had not re-enlisted like John.

She watched him walk up toward the barn, carrying the gun. And as she watched, Hannah had a sudden feeling that her helping this man, like all the other things she had tried to do for the war, would turn out badly, too.

Then she stamped her foot in anger at herself for thinking bad thoughts about John Porter.

Nervously she pushed her hair back from her forehead. She picked up the newspaper and read the piece once more. When she finished, she folded the paper neatly and put it back on the mantel.

Why does he need a gun if he hasn't re-enlisted? she wondered.

Why did he and the soldier crouch in the shadow of the Market House?

Why did he stand hiding the gun when I spoke to him?

For the rest of the day these thoughts tormented Hannah. And by the end of the day, when she stood at the window looking toward the lantern light in the barn, she knew that she alone must answer the questions. She alone must find out about John Porter, refugee. She had brought him to the house, she would have to find out whether he should stay.

"*We* do not break laws," she said softly to the lantern light. "*We* do not buy guns from soldiers. Why do you, John Porter? Why do you?"

CHAPTER EIGHT

"A Redcoat! A Spy!"

As the spring days lengthened and became brighter and warmer, Hannah kept watch. She saw John Porter leave in the morning; she waited for him to come back at night. She saw that sometimes he carried his gun. Then it occurred to Hannah that he carried his gun home to the barn at night, but that he did not carry it away in the morning. And then it came to her, in one blinding flash, that it could not be the same gun, but that it must always be a new one he brought home. So he must be buying more and more guns although he knew it was against the law.

One day, when it was almost time for Hannah to plant her garden, she went to the barn for some packets of seeds which were stored there. It was in the morning after she had seen John Porter leave. Hannah had decided that she would take a look around the barn as long as she was going up there. She had just stepped inside the barn door when a shadow fell on the floor in front of her.

Startled, she whirled around. It was John Porter!

"What are you doing?" he asked.

"Getting some seeds," Hannah answered. "It is time to plant my garden."

"Where do you keep your seeds?" He sounded cross.

"Father put them up here," said Hannah, walking over to a shelf on the opposite wall. "Here are all the seeds." She held them at arm's length for him to see.

"Is that enough for a garden?" he asked, looking at the little packets wrapped in old newspapers.

"I don't know," Hannah admitted. "It is all I

have. I shall have to see if it's enough." Then she stared at him.

He did not return her look, but said, "I forgot something. Will you wait here while I go up to the loft for it?"

Hannah suddenly felt very bold. "I would like to see your room," she said.

"Then come up with me."

Hannah climbed the ladder to the loft. Amazed, she looked around. It was clean and neat. Whatever hay had been left John had stuffed up the sides of the loft and under the roof and spread on the floor. In one corner he had a pile of it to sleep on with a bed sack on top and all the blankets and quilts they had given him on top of that. His lantern and his coat hung from a peg. The room looked comfortable.

"How do you like my home?" he asked.

"It is really very nice," admitted Hannah. She had worried about him sometimes during the long, hard winter. "Were you warm enough during the snowy days?"

"Yes," he said. "I didn't suffer from the cold."

While they talked, Hannah's eyes darted around the loft. Finally, in the farthest dim corner she saw a gun propped against the wall. One gun.

John Porter's eyes followed hers. He went over to the gun and picked it up. "This is what I forgot," he said.

It was on the tip of Hannah's tongue to accuse him, to ask him questions, to search through the pile of hay under the bed sack for other guns, but she dared not do any of these things. Instead, silently, she started down the ladder and John Porter came after her.

At the door they parted. He continued down the hill and Hannah went to her garden.

One gun, she thought. That is not possible. I have seen many more come in here. I *must* get up to the loft again and search his bed sometime when he is not here.

For several days after that Hannah walked up toward the barn each morning, but she always became frightened before she reached it and turned in to her garden instead.

One morning as she walked up the lane, John Porter stepped out from behind the huge rock at the entrance to the garden just as she approached it. Hannah was startled. She let out a cry and began to shake. She must have looked frightened, too, for he said reassuringly:

"I came to see if you had planted your beans yet."

"No. Not yet," said Hannah and, still flustered, she added, "I thought I saw you leave for the blacksmith's."

His face darkened. "Do you watch for me to leave?" His voice was sharp.

Hannah realized she had made a mistake. Quickly she said, "I happened to be at the door when you walked down the lane."

He did not answer her, or explain why he was there, and the look in his eyes bothered Hannah. She turned away. "Excuse me," she murmured, and brushed past him. "I have to plant my seeds today."

He left abruptly and Hannah began to put the seeds in the rows she had prepared for them.

Her mind seemed to boil with questions.

Did he suspect that she would like to search the loft? Was that why he was waiting in the garden?

With an effort, Hannah put her mind on the seeds. She worked hard. She planted corn and beans and squash. By the time the sun was showing over the roof of the house, she had finished. She was tired, not only from the work of planting, but from worrying about John Porter.

As Hannah stood up and gathered her tools together to return them to the barn, she made a decision. Right now, she thought, right now I will climb to the loft and look around carefully.

Her heart beat fast with excitement and with fright. There was no doubt about it: John Porter frightened her now just by looking at her. Hannah dared not think of what he might do if he found her up in the loft.

When she reached the barn, she hung the spade and the rake back on the row of pegs along the wall beside the scythe and the pitchfork.

How empty the barn is now, she thought, for their cow had long ago been eaten and their horse had been given to the army. No hay crop had been cut that year, either, so there was no delicious smell of new hay. The plow and the harrow stood in one corner and the oxbow hung on the wall. Everything was dusty from not being used.

It is altogether different this spring, Hannah thought to herself. The war reaches everywhere, even into our barn.

She looked out of the barn door again and as

far down the lane as she could see to make sure no one was coming, then picked up her skirts and climbed quickly up the ladder to the loft.

She decided to start with the pile of hay under the bed. She put her hands and arms into it up to her shoulders, through the sides, the top, the bottom, everywhere. Her hands touched nothing. Then she took the blankets and quilts off the bed sack. She felt that, too. Nothing. She shook each quilt and blanket. There was nothing there. Hannah pushed the hay together and laid the bed sack on it and spread the quilts over that.

No guns, she thought. Was I wrong, then?

She looked at the walls and realized that the two corner walls and the rough clapboards over the bed could hide guns under the hay that had been stuffed there.

Now she tore all the hay down from the walls and from between the beams of the ceiling. She could barely breathe, her heart beat so furiously. The dry hay was dusty and suddenly she sneezed! Stock-still she stood, holding her breath, afraid that her sneeze might have been heard by someone, afraid that she would be caught.

When the silence continued, unbroken by a

voice or a footstep, Hannah let out her breath in relief. Then she went on with her search, going over the walls, the corners, the rafters.

There were no guns.

Hannah's eyes filled with tears of disappointment. She had been so sure she would find them. She stood forlornly, trying to decide what to do next. The loft looked as if a horse had been tramping around in it; there was hay everywhere. Hannah knew that she must not leave it looking that way, so now she stuffed the hay back between the rafters, between the beams of the walls. With her hands she brushed all the hay from the floor into the corners. Then she walked to the top of the ladder and looked back at John Porter's room. It looked almost the same as when she had come. She climbed down the ladder and went outdoors. Her heart was still beating wildly.

She sneezed again. A piece of hay was tickling her nose. She looked down at her dress and apron and shoes and saw that they were covered with dust and bits of hay.

As she approached the big rock near her garden, she stopped and shook her clothes and brushed the hay off them with her hands. She took off her shoes and turned them upside down and shook them and put them back on. She took off her sunbonnet and smoothed her hair. She shook the bonnet to get the hay off it. It flew out of her hand and landed in the soil almost under the base of the rock.

As Hannah reached for it, she was startled to notice that the soil under the rock looked like the soil in her garden: freshly turned.

Why should this soil be turned? she asked herself.

She didn't have an answer to the question, but there flashed into her mind the picture of John Porter springing out from behind this rock as she had come near.

Had it only been today?

Could it be that he hid his guns *here?*

Hannah picked up her sunbonnet and put it back on. Quickly she ran back to the barn to get a shovel.

She began to dig frantically, for she could tell by the position of the sun in the sky that it was almost time to be home for dinner.

She had made only a small hole when her shovel hit something. She dropped to her knees and put her hands into the hole. It felt like leather! She put

her face down close to the hole. It *was* leather, and a long thong was attached to it. A leather apron, that's what it was, like the ones blacksmiths used! She pressed down on it. There were hard things inside. She tugged and tugged at the leather until her arms ached. Finally she managed to work an end free. She turned this end back and saw the barrels of one, two, three, *four* guns!

There was a small noise behind Hannah. Terrified, she remained as till as a statue, then, when the noise was not repeated, she slowly turned her head. A squirrel stood on his hind legs and blinked at her. Hannah smiled in relief. "They're not yours?" she asked him. At the sound of her voice he scampered away and she said angrily, "No. They're *his*. Even his blacksmith's apron is wrapped around them!"

Hannah turned back to the hole, took one more look, covered over the guns with the leather, threw the soil back in, stepped it down, then ran to the barn to put the shovel back. She was almost faint with fear and excitement.

She clapped her hands together to get rid of some of the soil on them, but it didn't do much good, they were very dirty. I must wash my hands, she thought.

And then the full meaning of what she had just found burst upon her.

He is a Redcoat, she said to herself. The one I wanted to help. He is a Redcoat! He is a spy!

"A Redcoat! A spy! A Redcoat! A spy!" Her feet seemed to strike out the words on the stones of the lane as she ran down to the house.

Quickly she washed her hands and face. She rushed upstairs and combed her hair. She put on a clean apron and a fresh cap. She came down to the kitchen and hung the kettle on the crane in the fireplace.

She did all the things she had been doing all winter, but she did them without thinking. Her mind was on one thing, and to think of that thing made Hannah sick. Again what she had tried to do to help had not turned out well. I brought him home, she thought, and now he turns out to be a Redcoat. A minute later, though, she had another thought. But if he *is* a Redcoat, I have a chance to catch him!

How to catch him? How to accuse him? When to accuse him? These questions went around and around in Hannah's head.

And there was another problem, too, that bothered Hannah. Should she try to catch John Porter all by herself or should she tell her brother John before he left with his company for camp?

When her mother came in from the hospital, Hannah looked busy. She hummed a tune under her breath. Outwardly she seemed calm, but her heart still beat fast and hard with excitement.

Her mother started to help her set the table. "Is the garden planted?" she asked Hannah. "Did you have a good morning?"

"Yes," Hannah answered, "the garden is planted. As to the morning," she added, thinking of her discovery that John Porter was a Redcoat, "you might say no. Or," she went on, thinking that now, by catching him, she could finally do a service for her country, "you might say yes."

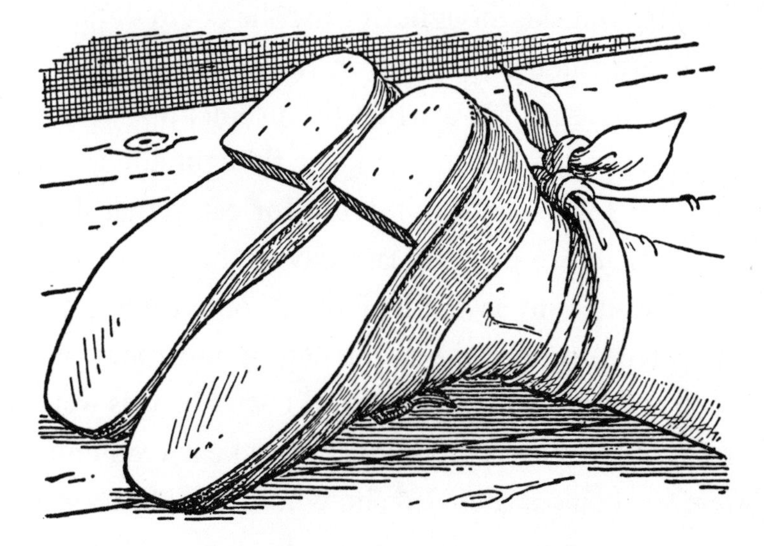

CHAPTER NINE

"... Thirty Dollars' Reward"

During the next few days Hannah's mood changed several times. Sometimes she was filled with joy at having found proof that John Porter was a Redcoat, sometimes with despair because she didn't know what to do with the proof or how to catch him. She thought again of telling her brother John or her father or her mother, but then she decided she wanted to capture this spy by herself. Day in and day out she thought of how she could do it.

There came a morning in May, though, when Hannah forgot for a while the problems that had been worrying her. Instead, she thought about her brother John who was leaving for camp that day.

Hannah wanted his last day at home to be a special one and so she had saved some hasty pudding from supper the night before and today she would fry it for John's breakfast. He was very fond of fried hasty pudding. To make it even more festive, Hannah decided she would serve it on her own pewter plate. She felt she was so close to doing a big deed for her country that she could take out the pewter plate and serve her brother's breakfast on it.

Early that morning she brought it downstairs for the first time in a year. She went down to the brook with it and picked some horsetail rushes and scoured it.

She hurried back to the house and washed and dried it. She set the table for John. Everyone else had eaten an hour ago. She cut the cold hasty pudding into pieces. She had found a bit of butter in the firkin and she put that in a long-handled frying pan which she rested on a trivet in the hot fire.

When the butter was melted, Hannah put in the hasty pudding.

Before long she heard John's footsteps on the stairs and he entered the kitchen, dressed in the buff-and-blue uniform of a private of the Continental Line. He had his knapsack, his canteen, his musket, and his powder horn. He carried his three-cornered hat. He put all these things down on a chair near the door to the borning room and turned to Hannah.

"Well," he said, strutting back and forth, "how do I look?"

Hannah smiled as she watched him. "You look handsome," she said. "Are you happy to be going back to join your company?"

"Yes." The way John said "yes" made Hannah look at him again. His face wore a thoughtful, faraway look and the "yes" was full of his wish to beat the Redcoats.

Redcoats, thought Hannah. *I* can catch *one* Redcoat.

"What are you cooking?" asked John, sniffing. He sat down at the table.

"Fried hasty pudding," said Hannah, turning the pieces to brown on the other side. "I saved some from last night's supper and you may eat it off my pewter plate." She crossed to the table and pointed to the plate. "Doesn't it shine?" she asked. "I polished it just now."

"Well, be quick," said John. "I'm hungry."

There was a sudden noise. The door flew open. John Porter stood on the threshold. He came one step into the room and stood, a musket in his hands.

Hannah and John both looked startled, for he had never come to the house like this before. They greeted him.

John Porter did not return the greeting. "So you're going back to fight the war again," he said, and there was something unpleasant in his voice.

"Yes," John answered, and again Hannah had the feeling that that little word was full of big thoughts.

"Do you like your uniform?" John Porter went on.

"Yes," John answered again. "I'm a private in the Second Rhode Island Regiment now, the Continental Line."

John Porter smiled, as if this information were humorous.

Suddenly Hannah could stand it no longer. John

did not know what all these questions meant. He did not know that John Porter was a Redcoat. But Hannah knew, and she felt sure he had come just to poke fun at John, perhaps to pick a fight.

At that moment all her uncertainty as to what to do about the guns and John Porter and how to do it vanished. She started to shake with excitement. *Now*, she thought, I must accuse him *now* while John is here. I must do it now.

Trying to control her shaking, she went to the fireplace and brought the frying pan to the table. She put it down and picked up the pewter plate, intending to fill it with hasty pudding. She looked at John Porter then and said softly, "Is that the gun you bought from a soldier?"

He shot her a look full of hate.

Hannah's brother stood up. "From a soldier?" he repeated. "That's against the law."

Hannah turned to him. "That's not the only one he has," she said, and her voice quivered with excitement. "He has many guns hidden under the large rock near my garden."

"Why, you, you . . ." John Porter stopped, then stood up to his full height. "Yes," he admitted, and his voice was calm. "I have many guns hidden at the rock. I supply my British brothers, who, like me, are pretending to be rebels."

John shouted, "Then you're a Redcoat!"

John Porter bowed from the waist. "You're correct this time. And I'm proud to be a member of His Majesty's troops." His voice rose. "And glad to make trouble for rebels wherever I find them!"

Hannah could barely speak, but she stammered, "Then . . . then, when you said you were John Porter, you did not tell the truth."

"No, ma'am." His voice was sarcastic. "I did not. I said my name was John because you said *his* name was John." He pointed to Hannah's brother. "I said Porter because I've been at New*port*."

"You were not wounded then?"

"Yes, I was. And captured by some rebels and brought to Providence as a prisoner of war and put into the hospital on the hill."

"An escaped prisoner of war!" It was John's voice saying it to himself almost. "That is why you were worried about my mother nursing there. You thought she had seen you and would recognize you. An escaped prisoner of war!"

"With a price on my head." John Porter took a piece of newspaper out of his pocket and waved it at Hannah and John. "You read the newspapers. You know all about buying guns from soldiers. How is it you didn't see this? It describes me well and then it says, 'Any person that will return said escaped prisoner of war shall have thirty dollars' reward by applying to the Adjutant General of the State of Rhode Island.' "

John said loudly, "I'll have that thirty dollars! And I'll have it soon!"

He started toward the chair where he had dropped his musket.

"You never will," shouted the Redcoat. "This is what I came for!" And he lifted his flintlock and fired.

It all happened in an instant. At the moment the Redcoat fired, Hannah screamed and jumped between him and John. As the roar of the gun filled the room, Hannah felt something hit her. She fell to the floor.

She lay unconscious for a few minutes. Then slowly she came to her senses. She was lying over near the door to the stairs and her left arm hurt badly. In a rush she remembered what had happened. She looked around the kitchen and saw

chairs overturned. Slowly she realized that there must have been a fight. She raised her head a little and saw John sitting on the Redcoat's chest. As she watched, he pulled a towel off the table and started to tear it with his teeth and one hand. She moved, and he looked at her quickly and grunted.

Shakily Hannah sat up.

"John," she asked, "are you all right?"

John nodded and took the end of the towel out of his mouth. "Help me," he begged. "I need strips to bind his hands and feet."

Hannah stood up. The pain in her arm was sharp. She wavered. Then she walked over to John and with one hand helped him tear the towel into strips. Together they tied the man's wrists and ankles while he squirmed and shouted. John got up then and took the straps from his canteen and his knapsack and bound them over the linen strips. Then he pulled the captured man to his feet, dragged him across the room to a large oak chair, pushed him into it, bound him securely to it. The spy began to shout at Hannah hysterically.

"It's *your* fault," he screamed. "Digging around rocks. Searching the barn. I knew you had been there. I waited until today so as to get you both together. Now look at me!" Tears of rage streamed down his face. Suddenly he stopped shouting and hung his head.

John turned from him to Hannah, who stood dumfounded. "Are you really all right, Hannah?" he asked.

"Yes," Hannah murmured, "except my arm. It hurts." In a daze she said, "But where is the bullet he shot at you?"

John walked over toward the borning room and picked up the pewter plate. "I don't know where the bullet is yet," he said; "it must be imbedded in a wall. But here is your pewter plate. It saved your life." He paused. "And mine."

Hannah looked at the plate in John's hands. On the bottom was a dent, where the Redcoat's bullet had glanced off it.

Hannah looked at John questioningly.

He explained. "When he lifted his gun to shoot me, you stepped between us and you still had the pewter plate in your hands. You must have held it close to you and the bullet hit it. The force knocked you down and hurt your arm. I guess then you fainted while he and I fought it out."

Wonderingly Hannah reached for the plate. She

turned it over and over and stared at the big dent in the bottom. The bullet had almost gone through it. "My pewter plate," she said. "John, it should have been melted down for a bullet. It should have been a bullet made to kill a Redcoat. And now, instead, it has saved your life. My pewter plate has saved a life!"

John grinned and patted her shoulder. "It has done a good piece of work this morning, your plate. And you, Hannah, you have done a good thing, finding his guns. Together we have earned thirty dollars' reward."

Hannah smiled. She felt as if her heart would burst with pride.

Then her eye was caught by the overturned frying pan on the table and the hasty pudding all over the floor.

John saw it, too. "Never mind," he said, "we don't have time for hasty pudding now, Hannah. I must take this—this escaped prisoner of war to the Adjutant General at once. Stay here with him. He's helpless. I'll get the guns. We'll all go together."

Hannah told John on which side of the rock the guns were hidden. She picked up the tongs from the fireplace to use as a weapon in case she needed one. Then she sat nursing her sore arm while John went for the guns. She was afraid of the so-called "John Porter," but did not want to show it. She needn't have worried about him. He sat motionless, his chin on his chest.

When John returned he untied the Redcoat from the chair and unbound his ankles so he could walk. Then they started down the lane toward the Towne Street. The pain in Hannah's arm was bad, but she smiled in spite of it, for she was happy.

Children followed them, and women, and soldiers, and soon everyone knew the story. Jennifer and Betsy and Priscilla were there screaming, "Hannah captured a Redcoat!"

The crowd grew larger and larger all the way to the Adjutant General's office. There Hannah and John delivered the guns and the escaped prisoner of war. Over and over John told their story, and always Hannah blushed, for he told it as if she had done it all.

Finally, when the Adjutant General offered them the reward, Hannah refused to take it. "No," she said, "I have my pewter plate. That is all the reward I need."

The Adjutant General smiled down at Hannah. Hannah smiled back at him. He called two soldiers to take the spy away and another to take the guns.

As Hannah and John left the crowd behind and started down the Towne Street, it seemed to Hannah that everything was different and brighter. She was able to think of something besides the Redcoat and his guns, able to notice things around her. There were the women with their baskets, walking toward the Market House. There was a young boy pushing a handcart, calling "Yarbs and greens!" A thundering sound up ahead grew louder, and in a minute the Boston stage passed them with a great clatter of hoofs and harness. Then the street was quiet again. When they turned into the lane, Hannah saw that the fields and trees were faintly green. It was spring!

Hannah remembered the spring before, when she and John walked up this same hill, when he spoke about enlisting. Now he was going away again to fight for his country, but she, Hannah Williams, had done something for the war, too.

John put her thoughts into words. "You have caught a spy, Hannah, and found his supply of guns. It was a brave thing you did."

"I couldn't have done it without you," Hannah answered. "Or without my pewter plate. Just think, John, if it had been melted down for a bullet, it might have saved a soldier's life. Now it has done that anyhow."

"Shall I hammer out the bottom and make it smooth again before I leave?" asked John.

"No," said Hannah. "No! No! I want it with the dent in it forever and ever!"

PART FIVE *Fall, 1779*

CHAPTER TEN

". . . Her Pewter Plate"

The summer passed quickly that year of 1779. Since the day in spring when Hannah and John had captured the Redcoat, the trees had budded and burst into leaves. Now, in October, those same leaves were red and gold and were beginning to drop from the trees.

The people of Providence had been uneasy about the war during the summer, for the news of the fighting in the South had not always been good. But they tried to keep their hopes high and everyone was eager for victory and the end of the war and freedom.

For years they had lived in terror of the British troops stationed so near, in Newport, but at the beginning of October the rumors flew thick and fast that soon the British would leave.

One day, when Hannah was playing jackstones with Jennifer on the rock at the foot of the lane she looked up the Towne Street and saw the Town Crier approaching. He rang his bell and, as usual, he stopped in front of the Eagle Inn. Immediately a crowd gathered. Out of nowhere they seemed to come.

Hannah could never see the Crier without getting excited, for who knew what terrible or wonderful news he might have? Now she picked up her skirts and ran with everyone else to the Eagle. The crowd was thick, but Hannah managed to wiggle through to the front.

"Hear ye! Hear ye!" the Crier began. "Whereas it appears very probable from the motions of the Enemy that they are about to evacuate Newport, the Council of War has passed a resolve forbidding all private persons to land there, to molest the inhabitants, or to take or destroy their property under any pretense whatsoever."

A cheer went up from the crowd, so loud that it seemed to Hannah it would wake the dead in the burying ground at the other end of the Towne Street. But she screamed as loud as the rest. She cheered until her throat ached. She took off her cap and threw it into the air; she danced a jig with a little boy who stood near. She and Jennifer hugged each other over and over again.

When, finally, the crowd quieted down, Hannah left and headed for the lane.

At first she walked quickly, half-running, so as to get home and tell her mother the wonderful news. But then her steps slowed, for so many things were going around in her head that she needed time to think.

First there was her brother John in Tiverton. Surely he will be crossing to Newport with the troops, thought Hannah.

Then there was her aunt Abigail in Newport. John would find her and send them news. Hannah felt sure of this.

Hannah thought of the British leaving Newport

and she remembered a black thundercloud she had seen during the summer, a cloud that had seemed to hang over their house for a long, long time, threatening rain. The British have been like that, thought Hannah, like a thundercloud threatening to burst.

The year of the dark cloud, thought Hannah. That's what it has been since I kept my pewter plate.

She thought of all she had experienced during the year just past and she said to herself, I will remember the year of the dark cloud forever.

Far below her, on the Towne Street, the Crier rang his bell and read his proclamation again on the street corner. And in the hearts of all the people of Providence there was joy at the news.

But the lightest heart in all the town belonged to Hannah Williams.

She climbed the lane to the house and told her mother the news, and then she began to clean the empty dresser. For Hannah had something she wanted to put on a shelf of the dresser again.

It was a pewter plate that had saved a life. It was a plate with the mark of a bullet on it. It was her lovely pewter plate!

BIBLIOGRAPHY

Bibliography

Abbott, Katherine M., *Old Paths and Legends of New England*. New York and London, Putnam's, 1903.

Adams, James Truslow, ed. in chief., *Album of American History: Colonial Period*. New York, Scribner's, 1944–1949.

—— *Revolutionary New England, 1691–1776*. Boston, Atlantic Monthly Press, 1923.

Arnold, Samuel Greene, *History of the State of Rhode Island and Providence Plantations*. 2 vols., London, D. Appleton & Co., 1878.

Bartlett, John Russell, ed., *Rhode Island Colonial Records*, vol. 3. Providence, Knowles & Anthony, 1858.

Chitwood, Oliver Perry, *A History of Colonial America*. New York and London, Harper & Bros., 1931.

Cowell, Benjamin, *Spirit of '76 in Rhode Island*. Boston, A. J. Wright, 1850.

De Robernier, Louis J. B. S., *The War in America, 1780–83*. Manuscript Journal, R.I. Historical Society.

Dow, George Francis, *The Arts and Crafts in New England, 1704–1775*. Topsfield, Mass., The Wayside Press, 1927.

Earle, Alice Morse, ed., *A Boston School Girl of 1771, the Diary of Anna Green Winslow*. Boston and New York, Houghton Mifflin, 1894.

—— *Child Life in Colonial Days*. New York and London, Macmillan Co., 1899.

—— *Colonial Dames and Goodwives*. New York, Macmillan Co., 1924.

—— *Customs and Fashions in Old New England*. New York, Scribner's, 1893.

—— *Home Life in Colonial Days*. London and New York, Macmillan Co., 1898.

—— *Sabbath in Puritan New England*. New York, Scribner's, 1891.

—— *Two Centuries of Costume in America*. New York and London, Macmillan Co., 1903.

Field, Edward, transcriber, *Diary of Colonel Israel Angell: 1778–1781*. Providence, Preston & Rounds, 1899.

—— *Revolutionary Defenses in Rhode Island*. Providence, R.I., Preston & Rounds, 1896.

—— ed., *State of Rhode Island and Providence Plantations at the End of the Century: A History*. 3 vols. Boston and Syracuse, Mason Publishing Co., 1902.

Fisher, William Arms, *The Music That Washington Knew*. Boston and New York, Oliver Ditson Co., Inc., 1931.

Gould, Mary Earle, *Early American Wooden Ware*. Springfield, Mass., Pond-Ekberg Co., 1942.

Hazard, Thomas Robinson, *The Jonny-Cake Papers*. Boston, printed for subscribers, 1915.

Kerfoot, J. B., *American Pewter*. New York, Crown Publishing Co., 1942.

Kimball, Gertrude Selwyn, *Providence In Colonial Times*. Boston and New York, Houghton Mifflin Co., 1912.

Laughlin, L. I., *Pewter In America*. Boston, Houghton Mifflin, 1940.

Lefferts, Lt. Charles M., *Uniforms of the American, British, French and German Armies in the War of the American Revolution.* New York, The New York Historical Society, 1926.

Lossing, Benson J., *Hours With Living Men and Women of the Revolution.* New York, Funk & Wagnalls, 1889.

—— *Pictorial Field Book of the Revolution.* 2 vols. New York, Harper & Bros., 1851–52.

Montross, Lynn, *Rag, Tag and Bobtail.* New York, Harper & Bros., 1952.

Preston, Howard Willis, *The Battle of Rhode Island.* Providence, R.I., State Bureau of Information, 1928.

—— *Rochambeau and the French Troops in Providence in 1780, 1781, 1782.* Providence, R.I., 1924.

Rawson, Marion Nicholl, *Of the Earth Earthy.* New York, E. P. Dutton, 1937.

Rider, Sidney S., *Rider's Historical Tracts, No. 6 and No. 13.* Providence, R.I., Sidney S. Rider, 1878 and 1881.

Staples, William R., *Annals of the Town of Providence.* Providence, R.I., Knowles and Vose, 1843.

Stone, Edwin M., *Life and Recollections of John Howland.* Providence, R.I., G. H. Whitney, 1857.

—— *Our French Allies.* Providence, R.I., Providence Press Co., 1883.

Weeden, William B., *Economic and Social History of New England, 1620–1789.* 2 vols. Boston and New York, Houghton Mifflin, 1891.

Wharton, Anne Hollingsworth, *Colonial Days and Dames.* Philadelphia, J. B. Lippincott, 1908.

MISCELLANEOUS SOURCES

(Hospital Papers, 1777–1782) R.I. Historical Society Collection.

Providence Gazette, 1778 and 1779. R.I. Historical Society Collection.

(Sermons by Rhode Island Authors, 1744–1902) Providence Public Library.